COLDINGHAM SANDS : J CAMPBELL KERR

WHERE'S THAT?

The approximate locations of our picture features

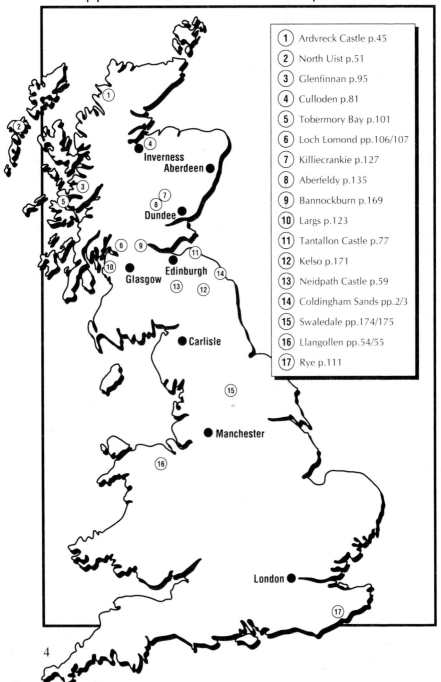

1. Ardvreck Castle p.45
2. North Uist p.51
3. Glenfinnan p.95
4. Culloden p.81
5. Tobermory Bay p.101
6. Loch Lomond pp.106/107
7. Killiecrankie p.127
8. Aberfeldy p.135
9. Bannockburn p.169
10. Largs p.123
11. Tantallon Castle p.77
12. Kelso p.171
13. Neidpath Castle p.59
14. Coldingham Sands pp.2/3
15. Swaledale pp.174/175
16. Llangollen pp.54/55
17. Rye p.111

Inverness
Aberdeen
Dundee
Edinburgh
Glasgow
Carlisle
Manchester
London

People's Friend Annual 1995

Contents

BACK COVER *The Round Tower, Windsor Castle.*

KRISTEN looked around the flat. It seemed strangely still, veiled as it was by dust. Yet she had been so happy here, and not very long ago, either. It was hard to believe, for now it was just a shell — and from the looks of things, Tom hadn't lifted a finger . . .

"Take what you want — anything," he had said, his indifference sharpening the ache in her heart.

She pushed aside the memory, along with her coat, and set to work. How could two people collect so much clutter in just eighteen months of marriage, she asked herself? Or so much pain, her heart whispered.

Pushing up the sleeves of her sweater, Kristen began to lift paperbacks off the bookcase and into a tea-chest. Her progress was soon stopped, though, by a little folded note which fluttered free of "Computers Today" and swayed to the floor.

She knew what it would say without reading it, but had to open it all the same with cautious, trembling hands. It was one of the many "reminders" she used to leave propped by the peppermill on the kitchen table.

Tom — popped out to the launderette — put the blue saucepan on a low light if I'm not back by seven — Kris.

Its abruptness came as a shock — had they ended up communicating without even a simple, scribbled "love you . . ."? Kristen could remember writing many notes like that on returning home from her office and feeling swamped by the chores awaiting her.

So by the time Tom came home, Kristen was often simmering more than the evening meal — simmering with resentment. But she always managed to keep it contained.

The trouble was, she began to shut herself off from Tom — and knew it. But by the time she could make an effort to talk, Tom had usually shut himself off from her, and often ignored her notes, as if he were silently protesting.

Remember The

No wonder they had agreed to separate. Kristen had moved back to her parents' house whilst Tom had temporarily moved into his brother's flat. The lease on their own flat was up at the end of the month, yet as the weeks dragged by, they still hadn't emptied the place. Now there were only five days to go and something simply had to be done.

Tom hadn't seemed to care — hadn't even rung her about it, and by the looks of things, hadn't moved a thing, either. Kristen had considered putting an ad in the local paper to sell the furniture, yet somehow, she couldn't bring herself to do it. She couldn't stand the thought of strangers picking over the small home she and Tom had worked so hard to piece together.

by
**SUZANNE
THORPE**

Happy Times

NOW it seemed they had to work just as hard to break it up — only Kristen felt she was alone in this particular task. What did it matter about the books — or the flat itself, even! If Tom didn't care about it, then why should she? And as if to unleash all the resentment she had stifled for so long, Kristen tossed the remaining books aside.

They careered over the coffee-table and smoothly knocked her white china elephant to the wooden floorboards. As if in slow motion, she watched it explode into pieces, another broken dream. Fighting back tears, she lovingly picked up the pieces and laid them to rest on the table.

"Elephants never forget!" Tom had said with a grin, when he gave it to her on their first wedding anniversary. That was before they had started to forget — each other's feelings, each other's needs.

"Let *him* do it — let Tom clear this mess!" Kristen said aloud into the empty room. Her words fell like dust, she snuffled a few rogue tears into a tissue, then reached for her coat.

They had agreed that she would do her bit to empty the flat in her lunch hours, and Tom after work. If he kept to that, he might, just might, do something that evening. After all, there were only five days left.

As she gave one last look around the room, the now familiar pang of loss pulled at her. From outside, rain hurled like pebbles at the windows, and for a moment she was haunted by the ghost of a memory . . .

The nights Tom had rushed in, smelling of fresh air, his eyes seeking hers before he even tugged off his mac.

Thinking of Tom, walking into the flat, wet, cold . . . and alone, was almost unbearable for her. So, rooting in her bag, she pulled out the tin of chicken soup she had intended to heat up there for her lunch. Placing it in the kitchen, she hesitated.

Should she leave a note for Tom — to make sure he had something hot before he started work in the flat? Somehow, she couldn't.

THURSDAY, and two more days to go. Kristen opened the door cautiously. Would the living-room be empty, except for a dozen or so well packed tea-chests?

The flat looked just the same, or nearly. There were signs Tom had been there, but by the looks of it he had just moved things around and put them back in different places.

Kristen fought back a wave of anger, until she noticed something else on the coffee-table, amid the books. Her white elephant, only now it was back together again, the glued cracks looking like grey veins. Oddly, it looked better, more real, and certainly none the worse for its ordeal!

Tom hadn't emptied the flat — he had obviously spent most of his time repairing her elephant, and Kristen didn't know whether to laugh or cry . . .

In the kitchen, she noticed the tin of soup had gone. The only signs of it having been there were the tin-opener and a little terracotta patch dried on to the worktop. Peering closer, Kristen realised the stain was blood.

She shook her head and smiled, imagining Tom's muffled curse when he cut his finger. He had always been accident-prone.

Perhaps the cut had been serious? Kristen looked around the kitchen for clues, but it was giving nothing away. If Tom had cut his finger badly, that would explain why he hadn't emptied the flat, but the uncertainty was frustrating.

As if to counter it, and actually *do* something, she fished a couple of plasters out of her handbag, leaving them by the tin-opener. At least she wouldn't have to worry about Tom cutting his fingers off now . . .

She set to work, wrapping in newspaper pots and pans, gadgets — anything her hands blindly laid hold of through her tears — filling box after box.

One of them, she reminded herself, had to care enough to do all this, but after what seemed a back-breaking and heart-rending age, but was in fact only fifteen minutes, Kristen was stopped by the footsteps outside in the hallway. A key grated in the lock and the door opened.

"Tom . . .?" For a moment Kristen was lost for words.

"I came to help," he said quietly.

"Help?" echoed Kristen. "Well you haven't exactly done much up to now, have you, Tom! The keys have to be handed in the day after tomorrow!"

"I did what I could," said Tom, struggling to stay calm.

"Why did you come here at lunchtime — you might have known we'd only end up rowing! And why didn't *you* empty the place — why couldn't you even care enough to do that?"

"Heavens, Kristen — don't you understand? It's because I care *too much* to empty the place — that's why! I just couldn't bring myself to pack *us* away in boxes . . ." Tom finished in a husky voice.

Seeing the tears welling in Kristen's eyes, Tom reached for the box of tissues on the coffee-table.

"Thanks," said Kristen, pulling out a bunch of tissues.

"That's the reason I came," said Tom.

Kristen gave him a puzzled look.

"Tissues," said Tom. "The wastepaper-basket was filling up with them. It was like . . . like seeing baskets full of your tears."

He hung his head, as if he thought she would find that silly. But Kristen was recalling her own feelings of helplessness on realising Tom had cut his finger. She laid a hand on his arm.

"Thanks, Tom," she whispered.

"When I said I came to help, Kris, to be honest I didn't mean help to split up our home. I meant help to try to piece it together. Don't you see, Kris — these past few days have shown that we do care!"

"But . . . but it's all such a mess," Kristen said hopelessly.

"Let's talk . . ." he offered.

WE'VE lost sight of the ways we *are* close." He looked at their clasped hands.

"Instead, we focussed on the ways we were growing apart — you shut yourself off from me, Kristen, and I hated that!" His eyes were on hers now, dark and pleading.

"You shut yourself off from me, too," Kristen reminded him.

Tom smiled — a sad little smile.

"Yes, I did, but I realise now that you needed more space away from the housework, to be yourself. And I was too busy to see that."

"You were working long hours for that promotion, so we could afford a house deposit," Kristen reminded him.

Tom nodded, then sighed.

"Yet I still came home expecting closeness on tap, the way you needed affection on tap. We were both disappointed . . ."

"We've been so hard on each other, haven't we, Tom?"

Tom smiled at her tenderly and squeezed her hand.

"Yes, we have," he said. "In fact we've been harder on ourselves than we have on this place!" He laughed softly.

"What can we do, Tom? We can't just switch on, have instant reconciliation on tap."

"No, we can't," Tom agreed thoughtfully. "But we could make a start here, do it bit by bit?"

"Packing the tea-chests?" Kristen asked cautiously.

"No — *unpacking* them!" Tom smiled.

They hugged each other tightly for several minutes, until Tom finally spoke softly into her hair.

"So, shall I ring the landlord — tell him we want to keep the flat on?"

Kristen's mind was in turmoil when over Tom's shoulder she caught sight of her white elephant. She moved her head to look at Tom.

"Yes . . . yes, Tom! It might be difficult for a while, but nothing can be worse than being apart."

The look in Tom's eyes told her he agreed.

"But we'll both have to pitch in," Kristen reminded him, with a mischievous smile.

"Don't worry, love, the thing that's going to get the most attention from now on is *us!*" Tom vowed, with a grin.

But Kristen still sighed as she glanced around the room, around a home half-abandoned.

Tom understood her sigh, but chuckled as he went to switch on the log-effect fire. Then rubbing his hands in anticipation, he said:

"Come on, love, let's get cracking — we've a life to piece back together here!"

Kristen scrambled off the sofa and helped Tom to begin unpacking the tea-chests. Yet even in the shambles all around them she felt marvellous — to be doing something together!

For although they had a lot of repair jobs ahead of them, their hearts were back in it, at last. □

THAT DARN CAT

by
BETTY
PUTTICK

L IZ pushed the last box into her car boot and slammed it shut, wondering if she had the sheer brute strength to be an antique dealer.

More of a junk dealer, she thought ruefully, remembering the motley assortment she was hoping to sell at the local "Trash and Treasure" fair that day.

There was an insistent tapping on the window next door. Liz was in a tearing hurry. Everybody had told her that all the dealers arrived early before the general public, and it was then you might be lucky and make a few sales.

But she could see Emma's rosy old face at her window, so suppressing a sigh, she went up the path to her door.

Emma was a dear, and the best neighbour Liz could have wished for, but she did wish she hadn't chosen this particular morning . . .

Emma opened the door, all smiles as usual, and Liz noticed she was clutching her large china cat.

"You're off to the 'Trash and Treasure' this morning, dear, aren't you?" she asked. "Put this on your stall, would you? Old Mrs Briggs always said it was valuable, and I think I'd rather have a bit of extra money than something I'm always expecting to knock over and break."

"Are you sure, Emma?" Liz asked. She knew the cat had been a legacy from Emma's rich employer. She'd been housekeeper and general help to Mrs Briggs for years until the old lady died the year before.

11

Without resentment, Emma had explained Mrs Briggs had always promised to leave her a thousand pounds in her will, but when the time came, Emma's share of her employer's fortune had been this china cat.

It was not a pretty thing, with its long neck and ugly, grimacing face. However, her recent study of various books about antiques had told Liz that cats similar to this one sometimes sold for a great deal of money. And it had belonged to Mrs Briggs, who was unlikely to own rubbish.

The responsibility of selling it was something Liz didn't relish.

"Don't you think it would be better to take it to a good antique dealer, Emma? You'd be more likely to get its proper value.

"I don't know what it's worth," she went on, "and the 'Trash and Treasure' sale is more for bric-à-brac, not valuable antiques."

Emma looked disappointed.

"Oh, please take it, Liz," she pleaded. "All I want is the money to put towards a new coat . . . If you could get ten pounds for it, I'd be happy."

"Oh, all right," Liz agreed reluctantly, taking the cat.

It was surprisingly heavy, rather dirty, and the faded ribbon round its neck looked as if it had been there for years. She knew Emma had kept it on top of her bookshelves, afraid to dust it very often in case it got broken.

Emma had admitted, laughing, that she had a well-earned reputation for breaking china so it seemed all the more odd that Mrs Briggs had given her this china cat.

Apparently she had always said it was a lucky cat, but although Emma had never grumbled about her disappointment, Liz felt she would have been a good deal luckier if her employer had kept her word and left her the promised thousand pounds for her retirement.

WHEN Liz reached the venue where the fair was being held, the car park was almost full, and the area was buzzing with activity. People were staggering from large estate cars carrying enormous boxes, and with a feeling of mounting excitement, Liz picked up her own carton and made for the door.

She could scarcely see over the top of it, and a young man came out of the hall, not looking where he was going, calling out to someone inside. They collided and Liz almost dropped her heavy load.

"Whoops! Sorry!" he said, putting out a steadying arm, his eyes quickly scanning the box Liz was carrying. "Be back in a minute," he continued. "Don't sell that cat till I've had a look at it, there's a dear!"

Liz got a quick impression of white teeth, a likeable grin and a pair of very blue eyes.

She paused a moment just inside the door, taking in the scene. The hall was crowded and most of the stalls were already arranged with a dazzling montage of china, glass and silver.

There seemed to be barely an inch to spare, the surfaces crammed with goods, shelves and coffee-tables and whatnots of every kind set up to display even more.

Thoughtfully, Liz threw her cloth over the trestle table she had booked, which now looked huge. The contents of her box wouldn't even begin to fill it.

The girl at the adjoining stall smiled sympathetically.

"You can take half a stall, you know," she confided. "You want to get it as full as possible. The more crowded it is, the more they like to poke around for bargains!"

Easier said than done, thought Liz, remembering how long it had taken her to get her stock together. She'd had a ruthless blitz on her own home for anything saleable, and had been hunting charity shops, jumble-sales and flea markets for the last month since she lost her job.

The firm she had worked for this past year had gone the way of many others, and this stall was an attempt to keep the wolf from the door while she looked for another job.

But as beady-eyed dealers and the first members of the public wandered past, giving her stall no more than a swift once-over, Liz admitted to herself that this was not likely to net her a fortune.

Then a large, unsmiling man paused and picked up a pretty little teapot. Liz had labelled it £5.

"Give you three-fifty, trade," he offered.

"Four?" Liz heard herself say, to her own surprise, and was soon wrapping the teapot up in newspaper in the approved manner. Trying to look unconcerned, she put the money in her pocket, and entered the sale in her brand-new notebook.

COFFEE?" said Jill, her new friend on the adjoining stall, bringing her a mug.

As they stood chatting, Liz realised that a woman had picked up Emma's cat and was turning it round in her hands and looking underneath. Then, without a word, she ripped off the faded ribbon round its neck. As Liz turned, ready to remonstrate with her, the woman smiled.

"Pity it's been damaged," she said smugly. Now that the ribbon was removed, Liz could see that there was a crack running round the neck, where the head had been broken off and clumsily stuck back on.

"I'll give you a fiver for it."

"I know the crack makes it less valuable," Liz replied, eyeing the woman's expensive clothes and her fingers covered with rings. "But I couldn't let it go for as little as that. Besides, I promised to keep it for someone else to see."

"Oh, yes? I've heard that one before. Five pounds is as far as I'll go — you'd be a fool to refuse it. I'll be back in half an hour."

As the woman moved away, Liz turned to her companion.

"That's a shame," she said. "I'm trying to sell the cat for a friend. I

The Farmer And His Wife

by John Taylor

MY memory isn't what it was — and that's the understatement of the year!

I'll be up in our top fields and see something on the land or passing up the Forth. I'll say to myself that I must remember to tell Anne but when I get back to her I've forgotten.

What made me think of this, when I was coming into the kitchen for lunch, was that Anne was on the phone, or rather just coming off, saying, "Sorry I troubled you."

"I'm certain that was Alice's number," she murmured . "I looked it up."

"Why don't you look it up and write it down, dear? That's what those old envelopes are for."

Let's face it, local telephone numbers are at least five digits, some up to six. If you have to add a code that makes four more. Now, who can look up ten numbers and remember them?

Well, I can't, so I save used envelopes and split them with a knife to make a neat edge. They are on the ledge near the telephone.

I write my telephone numbers down before pressing the buttons. The split envelopes are also useful for messages.

If I'm in and Anne is out, sure as fate some of her bridge-playing friends will ring.

"Ask Anne if she'll be my partner on Thursday, John."

"What's your name?"

But the other person has hung up.

"John, you're hopeless! Why didn't you ask her name?" Anne asks when she gets back. "What was her age?"

Well, I ask you, how can you tell that from a high-pitched woman's voice?

"Over fifty, dear."

---

didn't know it was damaged, and I don't think she did, either."

"If it was perfect it would be worth a lot," Jill said, "but as it is, you won't get much. She's a dealer, though. I wonder why she wants it? Even if it was expertly repaired, it would hardly make her a profit. Did you say someone else was interested?"

Liz looked round the hall and could see the young man she'd collided with over by the coffee stall, talking to another man.

"Yes, that man over there noticed it when I arrived, and said he wanted to look at it."

"That's David." Jill smiled. "He's got a shop in town. You'd get what it's worth from him, but, of course, he may change his mind when he knows it's damaged. Why don't you go and ask him?"

Liz walked over and rather hesitantly tapped David on the shoulder.

He spun round, looking surprisingly pleased to see her.

"I was just on my way to you," he said, "but I got waylaid. You haven't sold that cat, have you?"

"No," Liz said. "I've just discovered it's been damaged, so you may not be interested, after all."

David looked keenly at her disappointed expression.

"Now look here," he said. "If you want to make any money in this business, the first thing you have to learn is not to point out the

14

I know all her bridge friends are that!

The next half an hour is spent phoning around to see who rang in the first place.

The fourth person she calls responds with, "I rang — didn't John tell you?"

COMING back to my memory — or lack of it — we were going to a wedding in Kirkby Lonsdale.

We were well on the way to Biggar when Anne said, "Did you lock the back door, John?"

"No, you were last out. You did."

"Where are the keys?"

We stopped the car — no keys.

"Did you put them under the churn in the byre?" I suggested.

"No, I never saw them."

I'll save you the arguments between there and Biggar . . .

We agreed to ring Helen, a farmer's wife near at hand, but had to contact Directory Inquiries for her number. We rang and gave her a number where she could contact us later that evening.

She came on laughing so much she could hardly speak. We had not only left the door wide open, but left the keys in the door!

Who was to blame has never been settled to this day . . .

I'll never forget when the phone rang one night at 11 p.m. We were sound asleep.

It was our Mary just back from a three-day winter break in Northumberland.

"Mum, where did I tell you I had hidden the — "

She had put the valuable in a most unlikely place, so she thought, from anyone burgling the house, but she couldn't remember where.

Anne couldn't either. I hadn't been informed, and was not pleased at being woken up over something which could have kept till morning.

ANNE told me this story over breakfast one day. She had been chatting to one of her friends whose mother was a widow living in Crail. She was going with a friend to spend a few days at the Crieff Hydro.

She didn't have much in the way of valuable jewellery, but a gold chain, a brooch and a bracelet were irreplaceable to her as her Tom had struggled to buy them for her when they hadn't much money. Where should she hide them?

She made a wee parcel, brushed it with black boot polish and put it under the coals in her coal-scuttle in the living-room.

She sat enjoying her evening meal in the Hydro, when it struck her that her daughter might go to her house and light a fire for her coming home.

Urgent telephone call! At least she knew where she had hidden her valuables — our Mary hasn't found hers yet.

defects to a potential buyer. If there's something wrong with the cat you should let me find it out for myself."

"Thanks for the advice." Liz smiled. "It must be obvious that I'm a complete amateur. But I thought you might tell me what the cat's worth as it is. I've just been offered a fiver."

"Let's have a look, then." David said, shepherding her back to her stall.

JILL and the woman next to her seemed to be engaged in a heated argument, and as Liz and David came up Jill, looking red-faced and annoyed, turned towards them.

"Liz! Pat here tells me she's sold your cat to that dealer you spoke to. I was only away for a couple of minutes, taking the mugs back."

"I'm sorry if I did the wrong thing. She said she had come back to collect the cat and bring the money," an equally red-faced Pat protested, holding out a five-pound note.

"Oh, no!" David exclaimed. "We can't let her get away with this. It was Mrs Dean, wasn't it? I noticed her earlier on. Come on, Liz, we should be in time to catch her."

He grabbed Liz's hand and they made their way out of the hall as quickly as the crowds would let them, just in time to see a large estate car disappear out of the carpark entrance.

David laughed.

"This is fun," he said. "I know where she lives. Let's give her a surprise."

His amusement was infectious, and as they drove along in his car Liz found herself telling him about Emma's legacy.

"I wanted to get more than a fiver for her," she said, "but it may not be worth any more than that. Poor Emma — some legacy it turned out to be."

David looked thoughtful.

"I'm curious to know what made Mrs Dean behave like that. She must have been keen to get hold of the cat, damaged or not, and she knew you might not let her have it by fair means. But I think there's more in this than meets the eye . . ."

Liz stole a sidelong glance at her companion. There was something so warm and friendly about him that Liz felt as if she'd known him for years. She knew she would have hesitated to tackle the redoubtable Mrs Dean on her own, but with David on hand it was all turning into an unexpected adventure.

THEY drew up outside a large cottage on the outskirts of the town, and rang the bell. Mrs Dean answered, but when she saw Liz and David she made a swift attempt to close the door in their faces.

But David was too quick for her and they followed the reluctant dealer into her sitting-room where the cat, half out of its newspaper wrapping, sat on the table, glaring balefully at them.

Mrs Dean looked flustered.

"There's been some mistake," she snapped. "I thought you had agreed to sell me the cat."

"You know I didn't," Liz said. "You took it when I wasn't there and thought I'd simply accept the money and let it go."

"Well." Mrs Dean bridled. "I made you a fair offer. The cat is practically worthless in its present state. I just happened to fancy it, that's all."

David had moved over to the table, and picked up the cat. He raised his eyebrows when he felt the weight, and shot Mrs Dean a shrewd look.

"I think I'm beginning to understand why you fancied this cat so much," he said.

Mrs Dean flushed under her elaborate make up, and one be-ringed hand shot out to grab the cat back. It was all over in a minute. As Mrs Dean snatched at the cat, it slipped from David's hands and fell to the floor, where it broke into several pieces.

With a gasp Liz fell to her knees. But it was not the shattered remains of Emma's cat that she picked up. It was a small, soft leather bag that had been concealed inside.

Mrs Dean's face was a study as she watched Liz open the bag and tip out a shining heap of coins.

"Look! They're gold sovereigns!" she gasped.

"As soon as I felt the weight of the cat I suspected something like this," David said. "And so did you, Mrs Dean. Am I right?"

"Of course not," Mrs Dean said weakly. "How could I have known there was anything inside the cat?"

"You know enough about antiques to know that a hollow ceramic cat couldn't weigh anything like that." David smiled. "And when you saw that the head had been glued back on, you thought you might find something interesting."

"Thanks, David." Liz said as they drove back. "Thank goodness you were there to help me. As it is, Emma will have her thousand pounds after all."

"And more, besides," David said. "Her boss Mrs Briggs certainly had a strange sense of humour. Suppose Emma had never discovered the coins?"

"Well." Liz laughed. "Emma always told me that she had a well-earned reputation for breaking china, and I think it must have been Mrs Briggs' idea of a joke to hide the coins in the cat. She thought it would only be a matter of time before Emma dropped it. I can't wait to see her face when I give her the coins!"

David smiled. "I think this calls for a celebration. How about you and me taking Emma out to dinner?"

"She'd love that! It's all thanks to you that Emma will have her legacy after all.

"If you hadn't spotted the cat when I arrived this morning I might have sold it to the first person who offered me ten pounds for it."

"Well, I hadn't expected to do an Emma and smash it!"

"Thank goodness you did," Liz replied, looking down at the pieces of the cat in their newspaper wrapping on her lap. "But then, Emma always said it was supposed to be a lucky cat."

"Lucky in more ways than one," David said, smiling into her eyes as they drew into the carpark once again.

Liz suddenly felt quite light-hearted, and even a bit light-headed, too.

"Back to the stall," she said. "Let's hope I've been lucky there, too."

"I hope so!" David smiled. "But when it comes to antiques, remember the more you know, the luckier you get.

"That gives me an idea. I need some help in my shop, and you said you need a job. What do you think? Don't make up your mind now — we'll talk it over at dinner this evening."

Liz carefully gathered up the pieces of the cat. The head was still intact and as she held it in her hand she wondered how she could ever have thought it grotesque. Why, its smile was positively benevolent. She really must try to get it mended . . .

David opened the car door for her and Liz, still holding the cat's head, got out. They said you were a lucky cat, she thought, but who could have believed how lucky you'd be . . .

As she told Emma afterwards, it must have been a trick of the light, but she could have sworn the cat winked at her . . . □

All

Daniel had suggested the spell in the convalescent home.

"It'll do you good, Dad," he'd said. "They'll get you back on your feet in no time."

And he was, more or less. He'd made it all the way to the garden bench with the walking-stick, but his triumph was spoiled by the sight of Nurse Harris trotting across the grass with that wretched rug over her arm.

He was angry with everyone. Especially Daniel, who kept on at him to sell his house.

"Oh, Jeannie," he whispered. "What shall I do?"

He often spoke to Jeannie, even though she'd passed away five years before. It was as though she was always with him, watching over him . . .

He was still fuming when he saw the little boy emerge from the shrubbery. He was about six, with fair, untidy hair and freckled cheeks. But it was what he was doing that captured Sam's imagination. The child was going through the pockets of his dungarees.

S AM sat on the garden bench, glaring at the tartan rug which lay in a heap on the grass. He hadn't been able to throw it far, but it would be one in the eye for that bossy nurse when she came back.

"Let's tuck you in, Sam," she'd trilled as she'd draped the rug over his knees. "We don't want you getting cold, now, do we?"

He wouldn't mind being spoken to like that if he was old, but he was only seventy! The stroke which had robbed him of the use of his right leg had in no way damaged his mind.

Those Years Ago

by TERESA ASHBY

The boy had found a hole in his pocket and was looking at it in horror. What on earth had he lost?

Sam knew exactly how he felt. He'd once had a hole in his pocket, too . . .

SAM could see his mother now, standing in the kitchen, boiling nappies in the old copper. She had a scarf wrapped around her head and her cheeks were bright pink from the heat.

"Go down to Fry's, will you, Sammy?" she said. "There's a list and a florin on the table. And if you're quick you can buy yourself a farthing stick of liquorice with the change!"

Now that *was* a treat! Better than a penn'orth of chips or a broken biscuit! A stick of liquorice! He grabbed the shopping bag, stuffed the florin and the list in his pocket and made for the door.

"Watch you don't lose that two bob." His mother grabbed him by the shoulder. "It's all I've got to last me the week!"

When finally he reached the shop, out of breath and panting, Mrs Fry had grinned across the counter.

"Hello there, Sammy. What can I get you?"

He reeled off Mother's list. "Five pounds of spuds . . ."

When he'd finished, Mrs Fry helped him pack all his shopping in the bag.

"Oh," he remembered. "And a farthing stick of liquorice."

And he never, in all his life, forgot the feeling of complete and utter hopelessness he felt when he reached into his pocket for the two shillings and found nothing but a hole.

In desperation, he stuffed his hand right in, bending over until he was touching his bony knee. Nothing.

"That's one-and-a-penny-threefarthings," Mrs Fry prompted.

He looked up at her fearfully. She was no longer smiling. The friendly Mrs Fry was looking distinctly unfriendly.

"Sammy!" Mrs Fry bent over the counter. Her mouth was turned right down at the corners. "Sammy, have you lost your mother's money?"

He gulped.

"Take the shopping anyway," she said brusquely. "I'll put it down . . ."

"No," he said quickly. "Mum wouldn't like that."

"Sammy, you've got to eat," Mrs Fry protested. "Your mum's feeding that baby, and with another on the way . . ."

That was the first he'd heard of it. Another on the way! Mrs Fry was right, Mum would have to eat.

"What if I help you look for it?" Mrs Fry said kindly. "Mr Fry can look after the shop for a while."

So, clutching Mrs Fry's hand, Sam led her back the way he'd come.

Mrs Fry puffed and panted and had to keep stopping every so often to get her breath back — but she was looking! That meant it must be possible to find it.

Sam's heart was pounding, echoing around inside his head. He wasn't so much worried about the pasting he'd get as the fact that he'd let his mum down. She'd trusted him with a whole florin, and he'd lost it.

His eyes were stinging as he scoured the ground, so full of tears it felt as though they'd burst. Someone must have found it, picked it up. He could just see his mum's face when he told her . . .

He didn't even realise he was crying until tears began to trickle down his neck. He rubbed a grimy hand across his cheek, smearing it black.

If the family starved, if the baby went hungry, if Mum got sick, it'd be all his fault.

Then a miracle happened. Through the blur of tears he could see something shiny in the grass at the edge of the path.

Mum's two bob!

He started to chuckle softly as he remembered. Mrs Fry was so pleased that she gave him his stick of liquorice for nothing!

It taught him a lesson, though. He never went shopping again unless he had the money tied up in a handkerchief and tucked somewhere safe.

SAM came back to the present with a start, as he realised the little boy was glaring at him.

"Oh," he said quickly. "I'm not laughing at you!"

The boy had both his pockets turned inside out. Both had fraying holes in them.

"What have you lost, son?"

"'Ow do you know I've lost something?"

"An educated guess," Sam said.

"You've lost your blanket, mister," the boy said, picking up the offending tartan rug. "Do you want it?"

"Yes, please," Sam said.

PANCAKE DAY

THERE is nothing like tradition.
To brighten up the year,
But I get really panicky,
As Pancake Day draws near.

I'm not so good at pancakes,
They're much too thick or thin,
And when I try to toss them,
They end up in the bin.

But now I've found the answer,
Perfect pancakes there to sample,
Because my HUSBAND cooks them,
Why not follow my example?

Chrissy Greenslade.

The boy carefully tucked it around him.

"You're good at that," Sam commented.

"My grandad likes a rug on his knee. He sits by the fire and tells us stories when it's cold, and in the summer we sit out in his garden."

"That's nice."

Sam didn't know where he'd go. Back to the old house, he supposed. The garden was too much for him now and he didn't need all those rooms, but where else was there?

At least he'd be away from here and bossy Nurse Harris. The alternative, an old folk's home, just didn't bear thinking about.

But someone close had bigger worries than Sam. He looked into the big blue troubled eyes and saw what Mrs Fry must have seen all those years ago in her shop.

"What did you lose?" he asked softly.

The lips began to tremble, the blue eyes brimmed with tears and the freckled cheeks went quite red.

"I lost Grandad's ring!" he blurted.

"What did it look like?" Sam asked, feeling utterly useless as he scanned the wide expanse of grass.

"It was my grandma's eternity ring," the boy said. "I only said I liked it and Grandad said I could have it and it was too big for my

21

finger so I put it in my pocket and I thought it would be safe and . . ." He took a huge breath, choked on a sob. "Now Grandad won't love me any more!"

"What if I help you look for it?" Sam said, reaching for his walking-stick.

"We'll never find it!" the boy wailed. "I've been all over the place."

"Of course we'll find it," Sam declared confidently. Then, as he began to follow the boy's dewy footprints across the grass, he noticed something quite startling.

The "boy" had two long plaits down his back!

Boys, girls, it was hard to tell the difference these days!

The damp from the grass soaked into his slippers and his eyes weren't as good as they used to be, but Sam looked over every inch of grass.

It was a hopeless task. They'd never find the ring. He felt for the little girl — she had to face her grandad and tell him that she'd lost his wife's treasured ring.

She talked quite happily as they searched, telling Sam all about her grandad and how he lived in the sheltered housing complex just over the other side of the hill, and how she was born six years after her grandma died. She was even named after her.

Sheltered housing . . . Sam rubbed his chin. He'd seen the adverts in the local paper for the little development overlooking the lake where the Canada geese over-wintered. He used to go fishing there, years ago . . .

From what the little girl was saying, it was like a brand-new village. They even had their own little shop and manageable gardens at the back of the bungalows.

When he was too tired to walk any more, Sam sat back down on the seat and welcomed the warmth of the rug over his knees.

"Poor Grandad." The little girl began to weep. "That ring was all he had left of Grandma."

Sam felt like crying, too. He looked down at the ground, at the girl's dirty white shoes.

"No, it wasn't," he said gruffly. "He's still got you. What's that?" he said suddenly.

Something shiny had caught his eye.

"What?" She looked down, realised in an instant what he was talking about and poked her finger down the front of her training shoe. She brought her finger out with the ring on the end.

"It's Grandma's ring!"

It must have fallen through the hole, straight down her trouser leg and into her shoe. She jumped to her feet and danced round and round with joy.

Sam knew exactly how she felt. He'd done just the same when he had his mother's florin back in his hand.

"I'll have to go," she said suddenly, kissed him fleetingly on the cheek, then scampered off until she was just a little dot about to disappear down the other side of the hill.

Nurse Harris appeared and Sam felt cross that she had to remind him where he was. He'd enjoyed the company of the bonnie little girl.

Children, he had always found, didn't see an old, sick man when they looked at him, but saw simply a fellow human being. He loved children. There was no show with them, no pretence.

He loved having his own grandchildren come to stay, even if they did wear him out! Even that would be impossible in a home . . .

"You frightened her away!" he said crossly.

"Sam — you spoke!" she cried, her face lighting up.

He hadn't spoken since the stroke; not because he couldn't, but because he didn't want to. He was afraid to open his mouth in case all the anger and bitterness came pouring out, especially the anger he felt towards himself.

"You have a visitor, Sam."

Sam turned slightly to see Daniel.

"He's talking," she told Daniel. "We're very pleased with the progress he's making in physiotherapy and he's . . ."

"Don't talk about me as though I'm not there!" Sam shouted, shaking with anger.

There was an uncomfortable silence, a shuffling of feet on the gravel path. Daniel gave Nurse Harris a meaningful look and she hurried away, no doubt to boss someone else around.

YOU'RE looking much better, Dad," Daniel said.

"Am I?"

"Look, Dad, about selling the house . . ."

"No!" Sam clamped his mouth shut and put his fingers in his ears just as he did every time Daniel tried to raise the subject.

"Now, you're going to hear me out!" Daniel pulled his father's hands down and held them gently.

"We've been worried about you, very worried. We can't let you go back to the house. If Maureen hadn't come by and found you, you could have died! How do you think that makes us feel?"

"Guilty?" Sam sniffed, knowing he was right.

"Yes, guilty," Daniel replied truthfully. "We love you, Dad. We only want what's best for you . . ."

"I want to go back to my own home," he said stubbornly.

"Mum wouldn't expect you to go back there," Daniel said softly. "That big old house is too much for you."

Daniel's wife, Maureen, joined them and Sam saw the look that passed between them. It was a look of resignation.

"Maybe . . . maybe you should move in with us for a while," Daniel said, none too convincingly. "The boys could share a room and . . ."

"Put everyone out, you mean?" Sam spluttered. "Have the boys resent me for being there!"

"Dad . . ."

"If I moved in with you, it would mean giving up my independence and parting with all those little bits and pieces your mother and I collected . . . and some bigger things, too. Where would the piano go in your house?"

Maureen gasped. She knew as well as he did that there wasn't room for another adult in that house, let alone another adult's belongings.

"But the house . . ."

"Is too big, I know." Sam nodded, then, straying off the subject completely, added, "You know, when I'm a touch more mobile, I may well take up fishing again."

"What?" Daniel paled, visibly confused.

A T that moment, Sam's two grandsons came charging across the grass towards them.

"Hiya, Grandad!" Tom cried, flinging himself down on the bench beside Sam. "Are you better?"

"I want to sit next to Grandad!" his little brother wailed.

"All right," Sam shuffled along. "Here, there's room for one each side!"

He put an arm around each of them and hugged them tight.

"Are you going to live with us, Grandad?" Tom demanded.

"No," Sam said. He was quite enjoying teasing his son, but enough was enough. He picked up his walking-stick and pointed it towards the hill.

"If I got dressed, could you drive me over there?"

"Of course," Daniel agreed at once. "Why?"

"Oh," Sam said lightly. "I've been chatting to a friend of mine who tells me that there are some nice little bungalows . . . I'm just having a look, mind!"

"Lakeside, you mean?" Maureen's eye-brows shot up.

"Can we come and stay if you live there, Grandad?" Tom said.

Sam chuckled. It would be nice to keep his independence, his treasured piano, and yet have the reassurance of knowing someone was close by . . .

"Oh, most certainly," he said. "Give me a hand up!"

The boys helped their grandfather to his feet, then walked back towards the main building, each holding one arm.

"What do you make of that?" Maureen smiled.

"I don't know!" Grinning, Daniel rubbed his hand through his hair. "And I wonder who this mystery friend of his is?"

"Oh, you can be sure it's a female." Maureen laughed softly. "Come on, let's bring the car round — before he changes his mind!"

Maureen set off towards the carpark, leaving Daniel more puzzled than ever. Finally, he ran to catch up with her.

"A woman, you mean?" he said, bewildered. "My dad?"

"He's full of surprises." Maureen smiled. "But I wouldn't have him any other way!"

"Know something?" Daniel said, laughing. "Neither would I!" □

WHAT you have to do, Beth," said her husband sensibly, "is learn to say no!"

Their son Peter laughed. "She's left it too late, Dad!"

Beth looked at him with less than her usual degree of affection. Peter was leaning back in his chair, his lanky, sixteen-year-old legs sprawled out over the fire-side rug.

"All you have to do is say thank you," he continued airily. "It's no big deal."

"It is to me!"

Beth Hume stood up and began gathering the dishes from their various resting places round the room. Life must have been a lot easier in the old days, she often thought, when families ate round a table, instead of having meals on their knees.

However, the TV set was off for the moment, and she

NEVER AGAIN!

by MARGARET BLACK

had the undivided attention of her family.

"After all, I am the vice-president." She moved a finger to avoid the mustard Roy always left on the side of his plate.

"Why did you agree to do it, Beth, if you dislike it so much?" Roy asked.

"Because I was asked, of course."

"But you must have known you would be expected to give a vote of thanks, and you know you don't like speaking in public."

Beth Hume maintained a dignified silence as she carried the plates into the kitchen. She knew perfectly well she should have refused office in the Wednesday Club, but she had been flattered.

It was an honour, she felt, and not too many honours came the way of Beth Hume. She was more likely to be found washing dishes in the hall kitchen than sitting up on the platform.

Her daughter Carole often complained about that.

"You always take a back seat, Mum — and you're as good as anybody and better than most!"

Beth remembered, squeezing washing-up liquid into the basin, how she had laughed at that.

"You sound exactly like your grandmother."

Carole laughed, too, her round, freckled face lighting up. It always seemed unfair to Beth that Peter had all the good looks, and him a boy, while Carole was red-headed, freckled and chunky. She was quick tempered, too, and always championing someone or something.

At the moment it was her mother.

"All you have to do is make up a little speech and learn it off by heart. Flatter the speaker. Say she's the best you've ever heard."

"But that might not be true —"

"Oh, Mum — who worries about the truth! This is a vote of thanks! Just remember the speaker's name, say she looks nice and sounds nice, and that's all there is to it."

"I wish you were doing it." Beth sighed.

"I'll write it for you, if you like."

But Beth shook her head firmly. She wrote her own little speech, learned it off by heart and hoped for the best.

The best was not to be. Half an hour before she was due to leave the house, there was a phone message from the president saying she had unexpected visitors and wouldn't be coming.

Beth turned from the phone in a state of panic.

"That means I'll have to take the meeting myself. I can't do it!"

"May will help you. She's a good secretary," Roy said soothingly.

Beth shook her head, her hand tight on the piece of paper on which she had written every word of her vote of thanks.

"You'll manage, Mum. Like I told you, no big deal — nothing to it!"

"Don't talk rubbish, Peter," snapped Beth, sorely tried.

"If you like, I'll run you along to the meeting," Roy offered.

"And I'll come for you, Mum," Carole was a new and very enthusiastic driver.

Never Again!

BETH arrived at the hall early. The hall-keeper had forgotten to put out the seats, but the heating was on and for that she was thankful. She set about dragging the chairs into place.

"You should have waited for me." May Downie arrived, breathless, with a bunch of chrysanthemums, and thrust them hurriedly into a vase. Floral Art was not her thing, but Beth was beyond worrying about flowers.

She set the last chair in place, and sat down on it to catch her breath.

"I had a phone call from the speaker, May. She'll bring her own projector, but she needs a screen."

May Downie's sparse brows flew up towards her neat brown hair.

"Why on earth didn't she let us know sooner? I'll run across and see if the Youngs are in. Bert's good at lending his."

"The Youngs are out." Beth stood up and found her knees were still shaking. "I've tried already."

She felt her heart beating uncomfortably as May vanished from the hall in search of a screen. The evening was surely going to be a disaster.

People were already arriving. Beth pinned an over-bright smile on her hot face and started welcoming members at the door.

May Downie came panting back and whispered that she had managed to locate a screen and that it would soon be on its way.

She also whispered, more heatedly, that the person responsible for bringing the milk had forgotten it, and did Beth know that the fuse had gone in the kettle again?

Beth did not.

If I get through this meeting, I'll never take another — not if I live to be a hundred, she told herself, her sheaf of papers dropping through her nerveless fingers. But a commotion at the door at least announced the arrival of the screen.

The speaker was five minutes late, by which time Beth felt as if the end of the world was near. As the door opened, she looked up, aware not only of being nervous but also that she was short, dumpy and red-faced. This stranger, this tall woman with the smart clothes and beautifully styled hair, was both strikingly good looking and very much at ease.

Beth stepped off the platform and went to greet her.

"Mrs Renton?"

She nodded. Her hand was cool and strong.

"I'm Beth Hume. This is Mrs Downie, our secretary," Beth stumbled through the introductions, convinced she was doing everything as badly as she possibly could.

When she finally sat down and heard Mrs Renton begin speaking with obvious confidence, Beth relaxed slightly.

As she listened, she became aware that there was something vaguely familiar about the woman, although she couldn't place what it was.

Finally the talk was over, the vote of thanks given and applause filled the hall. A kettle had been borrowed and milk produced from a helpful hall neighbour, so tea was brought in.

Beth realised her throat was drier than ever, and swallowing a sardine sandwich quite beyond her. She handed the plate to Mrs Renton, the sense of familiarity persisting, while May began rolling up the screen.

"I know you," said the speaker suddenly, leaning forward. "I've been puzzling all evening and I've just realised who you are. You're Beth Munro. I was Evelyn Grant — I was at school with you." She laughed, throwing back her smooth black head. "How many years ago was that? Too many!"

"Of course. I remember you now." Beth smiled naturally for the first time that evening. "I've been puzzling, too. It must be all of twenty-five years —"

"Don't tell me," protested Evelyn Renton, holding up her hand. After that, it was easy.

"My son David is coming back to drive me home." Evelyn Renton picked up her handbag. "He should have arrived by now."

"Carole is coming to collect me. She's my daughter." A real smile spread over Beth's face. "It's been such a pleasure meeting you again —"

She broke off as May Downie rushed over to them, her cheeks pale.

"There's been a slight bump outside with the cars, Beth. No-one hurt, but I'm afraid Carole —"

BABY'S FIRST CHRISTMAS

*WILL your eyes gaze wonderingly
  At the winter show?
As did other Baby Eyes,
  Long, long ago.*

*Will you see the Silver Star
  On your Christmas Tree?
As He saw the Guiding Star
  Bright with mystery?*

*Will His life inspire you
  As your years increase
With a love of loyalty,
  Brotherhood and Peace?*

Gaye Wilson.

Never Again!

HARDLY aware of having moved, Beth found herself outside in the darkness. She could hear Carole's tremulous voice, pitched higher than usual.

"I'm so sorry! It was my fault. I'm not good at reversing. I didn't see you in the dark. I'm sorry —"

"It's all right," a male voice said soothingly.

In the light now streaming from the open hall door, Beth could see the owner of the second voice, a broad-shouldered young man in an anorak, walking round to the back of his car.

"You've dented your bumper and broken the glass in your brake light," he announced.

"What about your car?"

"Nothing much that I can see. Just a scrape. Yours is worse."

"Dad'll have a fit. He guards the car like the Crown Jewels!"

The young man put his hand on her arm.

"Come into the hall and sit down. You're shaking."

Beth came to life again and suggested a glass of water. David Renton said he would drive Carole's car home for her and come back for his mother, but Beth suggested she should come as well, and they would all have a cup of coffee. No-one disagreed with her.

"What a night, Evelyn," she murmured, as they got into the back of the car, and she heard Carole sniffing miserably in the front seat. "It's the first time I ever took a meeting, too."

"You were fine — and it won't be so bad the next time."

Beth blew her nose.

"There won't be a next time," she declared flatly.

★ ★ ★ ★

Six months later, Beth came home from the business meeting of the Wednesday Club to find Roy alone watching the news. He switched off as she closed the door.

"Peter's at the disco and Carole's out with David Renton." He paused. "Again!"

"Mm." Beth slipped off her shoes and wriggled her toes luxuriously.

There were pink carnations in a vase on the coffee-table — a gift for her birthday yesterday — and the cat was stretched out under the television. Roy was in his shirt sleeves.

"She's seeing a lot of David Renton, Beth. Too much, if you ask me. He's getting to be a fixture around the place."

"Mm," murmured Beth for the second time, massaging her ankle.

"You're not showing much interest!"

"Of course I'm interested. It's just that —" She paused and her smile widened. "Mrs Fedden's retiring. I was proposed as the new president of the Wednesday Club — proposed, seconded and voted for unanimously."

"Good for you!" Roy grinned. "What did you say?"

"I said no, of course, but —" Beth's eyes sparkled in her round face, and she gave a great sigh. "Oh, Roy it was so nice to be asked!" □

by PAMELA HUTCHINGS

Rain, Rain Go Away...

"S ORRY, son, but it doesn't look like as if I'm going to be able to come, does it?" Mum said, sounding pretty fed up as she spoke to me on the phone.

I could only agree, my heart having sunk into my boots as I'd listened to her tale of woe over her sprained ankle. I handed the receiver over to Emma so she could speak to her gran. I could tell from the child's voice that she was terribly disappointed and I knew Adam would be, too, when he got home.

I told Mum to look after herself and get better in time for our holiday, and then felt Emma's arms around me.

"It's a shame Gran still has to live in Derby, isn't it, Daddy?"

I took her into the lounge and we curled up together in my armchair.

"That's where she's always lived," I explained quietly. "She doesn't know anyone down here — except us, of course. And Auntie Jane's in Derby, too . . . she isn't alone."

"But we are, and Auntie Jane's got her family. There's only us," Emma pointed out, tears in her eyes.

I pulled her closer. I, too, had felt low since Sue had died eighteen months ago.

I'd moved south with my job and met Sue while she was over from New Zealand on holiday. We'd stayed down here after we'd married and later found our dream cottage in the country.

Poor Sue. She'd lived in it for just a year before those fatal few months. I tried to hold back a sob myself as the memory threatened to overwhelm me again.

How we'd loved the cottage, making plans and growing all our own vegetables and fruit. Now the place was beginning to get me down. With the hottest July on record seeming to exhaust me, I was finding it difficult to cope with my job, the eight-year-old twins' demands, and keeping the house and garden tidy.

"We're taking Granny on holiday with us to that nice apartment we had last year," I reminded Emma. "You're looking forward to that, aren't you?"

"So long as she doesn't sprain her other ankle," she retorted.

"She couldn't help it, love. She didn't do it on purpose," I reasoned.

Emma looked thoughtful, her tears having subsided.

"No, but what about our birthday treat tomorrow? We can still go to the zoo and have lunch out, can't we?"

"Of course," I assured her.

But I must admit, I was already beginning to wonder if the zoo was the best place in this heatwave. There was no doubt it would be crowded on a Sunday, but then so would everywhere else, especially the coast.

I put my doubts to the back of my mind, realising that I would now have to slip out to the shops. Mum had been going to bring the birthday cake she'd made for Emma and Adam, and finding a replacement at such short notice on a Saturday morning wasn't going to be easy.

I quickly checked the fridge and kitchen cupboards to see what else we needed for our special day. Having already done my late-night shopping that week, I wasn't too pleased at the prospect of having to go through it all again.

"You don't really want to come with me, do you?" I asked Emma, trying to dissuade her so that I could make my purchases in secret.

"Yes, I do," she said quickly. "But if you want me to stay in the car, I will."

I smiled. She had guessed what was going through my mind. It wouldn't have been so bad if Adam had been there, too, but he was over at the Scout hut in the village where the Cubs were helping with their jumble sale. I couldn't leave Emma alone. And she hated staying with a neighbour.

In the end, I bought a large sponge cake, some icing sugar and candles, and vowed to see what I could do to it later when the children were in bed. The rest of the shopping, with Emma's assistance, was easy.

I knew there were quite a few jobs to be done around the house, but I felt the garden was most in need of attention. At this rate the vegetables wouldn't be worth eating.

But as we drove home great drops of rain splashed on the windscreen. We'd only just got inside when we heard thunder.

"Granny wouldn't want to have travelled in this," Emma stated thoughtfully, clinging to me as torrential rain belted down.

The garden needed water, but this was ridiculous! Already a torrent was gushing down the road from the top of the hill.

Emma followed me into the bedroom as I hung up my jacket in the wardrobe.

"Adam will be soaking wet."

"Well, I've no doubt there'll be others in the same boat," I said, trying to ease her concern for her brother.

"Maybe we'll need a boat, Daddy," she retorted, looking out of the window at the sodden world.

I smiled, but could see her worried expression as she stood with her nose up against the window pane. The twins were very close. Although they fought like cat and dog when they were together, driving me mad at times, they always protected each other when there was trouble.

Their birth seemed like only yesterday. I could remember how absolutely thrilled we were to get one of each. "Our instant family," we called them. Sue would have been so proud of them now that they were eight years old.

I WAS just thinking about preparing lunch when there was a ring at the doorbell. I opened it to a young woman standing on the step, looking very bedraggled.

"I'm sorry," she began. "I've broken down . . . I mean my car has, and I can't shift it."

"You'd better come in," I told her. "You're drenched."

As she entered, dripping over the hall carpet, Emma appeared.

The girl smiled at her as she followed me into the kitchen and stood on a mat. I handed her a large towel, which she accepted gratefully.

"Oh, thank you. I'm really worried about my car. With that water rushing down the hill I was skidding all over the road. The only way I could stop it was by driving it into the hedge!" She began towelling her dripping hair. "I'm sorry to be such a nuisance."

"Don't worry about it. I'll just take a look," I said, slipping upstairs again to get a better view from my window. The problem was obvious.

"The car's certainly well into the hedge," I agreed, as I came back to the kitchen clutching my bathrobe. "I think you'd better get into this. Come on, Emma. We'll get out of the way."

As I closed the kitchen door behind us, Emma looked very concerned.

"She looks frozen. She'll catch a cold," she announced, in her usual very loud whisper.

"Then we'll have to give her a hot drink, won't we?" I said.

She smiled.

"How about soup? We were going to have lunch and we could have it in a mug . . . just like we always do, Daddy," she suggested, tailing off as the door opened and the girl appeared.

"I've put my clothes round your boiler, although it's not on, of course," she stated.

"At this time of year we just put it on to heat the water. But I'll put it on now. It doesn't take long to heat up. We haven't been using it much in this hot weather."

With her tousled hair, she looked much as Sue had done when she came out of the bath.

"I'm sorry to land myself on you like this. I really only wanted to ask if I could use your phone," she said.

"You're welcome to, but I warn you that until this storm subsides and your brakes have dried out, you won't be going anywhere. You're a captive . . . so how about some lunch? It's nothing grand, I'm afraid."

She smiled. "Thanks. That would be nice."

"And I'll try to help you get your car going later. Even the AA couldn't do any more for you right now," I reasoned.

"I don't suppose they could," she agreed, "but at least let me help while I'm here."

I WAS grateful to her as she buttered the bread for the sandwiches while Emma emptied tins of soup into a saucepan.

"It's chicken," she stated. "I hope you like it."

"Anything would be welcome," the young woman said with a smile. "I'm Gill Buckstone, by the way."

"Dan Richardson," I offered. "And this is Emma, and there's also Adam. They're twins."

"It's our birthday tomorrow," Emma stated.

Trust children to announce it from the rooftops, I thought.

"Your birthday!" Gill said, suitably impressed.

"And Granny was supposed to come today, and now she can't because she's sprained her ankle."

"What a shame! How old will you be?"

"Eight. And I would have liked my mummy to be here."

Gill shot a glance at me.

"Sue died nearly eighteen months ago," I told her.

"I'm sorry," she said quietly.

As she cut the sandwiches I couldn't see a ring on her finger. Then I chided myself for being nosey and refused to give in to the flicker of curiosity which was growing inside me.

"I'm going to take these into the lounge," Emma announced, taking the plates. "We can put the fire on in there and have a picnic lunch."

Gill laughed.

"Oh, dear, it's not that cold now, is it? I mean, I don't want you to swelter . . ."

"We can turn it off when you're warm," I said, following my daughter, balancing the tray with the mugs of hot soup. "I'm afraid I should have picked up Adam by now. I'll just phone."

I couldn't find the number of the Scout hut, so I rang the Scoutmaster's house. It seemed all the boys were there and being given lunch. I promised to collect him later.

But the storm hadn't any intention of easing and when at last I looked out of the window upstairs, I could see that the water looked even worse as it ran down the hill.

"I'm sorry, but you're in for rather a long wait," I told Gill.

"So, you'll have to stay for tea," Emma added quickly, a big grin of delight spreading across her face.

Historic Scotland
ABERFELDY

A BERFELDY, on the south bank of the River Tay, has three very notable features.

The first is General Wade's bridge over the river, reckoned his masterpiece in bridge-building. The second is the Memorial erected in Queen Victoria's Jubilee year (1887) to commemorate the raising of the Black Watch, 42nd Regiment of the line, in 1739. The third is the nearby Moness Burn, considered by many to be the finest waterfall-stream in Scotland. Each in its own way is admirable.

General George Wade's bridge, the subject of my drawing, dates from 1733. Around that time, in the aftermath of the 1715 Jacobite Rising, the General built a number of great military roads in the Highlands as part of a "Pacification Scheme" to give easier movement to troops in keeping a watchful eye on the Highland clans.

Aberfeldy Bridge was the last and finest Wade built, and in designing it he was helped by the notable architect, William Adam. My drawing was made from the south side of the river.

Many so-called "Wade Bridges" were, in fact, built by his successor, General Caulfield. But the amiable Caulfield would not resent Wade stealing his thunder. It was he who wrote the well-known lines —

*"If you'd seen these roads before they were made,
You'd lift up your hands, and bless General Wade."*

"My brother owns a tractor and he'll get me out of there in no time," Gill told me. "He married my best friend from school . . . Cindy and Geoff. Their name is Buckstone as well, of course. Do you know them? They live at Meadow Farm at the bottom of the hill."

I shook my head. "I know the farm, of course, but I haven't met them."

"I visit them during my breaks," Gill offered. "I'm a nursing sister at the County Hospital. Mind you, it's not that often I get the chance to come because I don't get that much time off. It's difficult with all the staff shortages."

I knew all about that. When Sue was ill, I'd been amazed at the long hours the staff had worked.

"Now, we won't be able to go to the zoo tomorrow," Emma grumbled, getting her oar in again. "With no Granny and no zoo . . . it'll be some birthday!"

Gill took her hand.

"It might be sunny again by tomorrow. This is only a flash in the pan," she comforted, but even she looked doubtful as the rain pelted against the window.

HOWEVER, by five, the rain had eased off considerably and I could see that Gill was growing restless.

"I do have some clean clothes in the car . . . that's if someone could go out and get them for me. I'm sorry it can't be me," she said looking down ruefully at the bathrobe.

I had to smile.

Slipping into my boots, I squelched through the mud that had come from the farm next door on to our drive and made my way to the car against the reduced torrent of water. I let myself into the abandoned car and tried the engine. I knew it was a foregone conclusion that it wouldn't start, but I felt I ought at least to try. I trudged back with the bag Gill wanted.

"I rang Geoff and he said he'll deal with the car later. He's had the animals to cope with, and then some of the farm buildings are flooded. I must go and help."

I nodded, disappointed to lose her so soon. "I really must go and collect Adam. He'll think he's been abandoned!"

I felt sad as she slipped upstairs to dress. I was being selfish, I knew, but I didn't want her to go and was trying not to show it. However, Emma was never one to be slow in coming forward, and when Gill came downstairs looking absolutely stunning in blue slacks and a matching shirt, she said what I was afraid to.

"I wish you didn't have to go."

Gill smiled, putting her hand on Emma's shoulder.

"I hope this won't be goodbye," she said.

"You can come to tea tomorrow," Emma invited.

"That's very kind of you. Now, I really must go."

Emma quickly put on her boots and the three of us trudged down the hill, making our way towards the village where people were mopping out houses. It was then that we realised the extent of the damage. The houses at the bottom of the hill were much worse off than us.

As we got closer we could see the Scouts and Cubs had been put to work. We found Adam with his trouser legs rolled up, paddling around in bare feet with a mop and bucket. There was a general air of comradeship and the boys actually looked as if they were enjoying themselves.

"Well, at least, he's doing his good deed," Gill said, laughing with us. "Many thanks for all your help," she added, her eyes meeting mine.

Our gaze held for a moment, and then I watched her walk on.

THERE'S no doubt that I wasn't the only one thinking about Gill as we all strolled home after helping our neighbours.

"You know, you didn't even ask her where she lives," Emma said, sounding quite cross.

Adam was eyeing me curiously, waiting for my reaction to this.

"She'll have to collect her car," he reasoned, pointing to it.

I nodded. Even I had managed to work that out for myself, and found myself keeping an eye on it. However, it was about nine o'clock that evening before I saw the tractor arrive and I went out to help. Apart from a few scratches on the bonnet, the car was fine and started after a few tries.

"See you later, Geoff," Gill said, as he got back into his tractor. He smiled from high up in his cab and drove off.

"I've brought a couple of small offerings," Gill said, handing me two hastily-wrapped parcels. "I hope you don't mind."

"Emma invited you to tea tomorrow," I reminded her. "Oh, no! Their birthday cake! I haven't decorated it yet!" I said with a groan. I'd spent so much time thinking about Gill, I'd completely forgotten about it.

"Now there's a coincidence." Gill laughed. "I sometimes do a hasty job of cake decorating for the children on the ward."

"And so you'll stay and help?" I asked.

"If you'll let me?"

"If you'll let me!" I echoed, unable to believe my luck. "Oh, yes . . . please."

" And the zoo . . . you don't fancy that, too, do you? Weather permitting, of course."

"It's been ages since I went to a zoo. I was hoping you'd ask," she whispered, her eyes holding mine.

"You know, Gill, the moment I saw you standing there on the doorstep I felt that you'd been sent as an angel of mercy . . . for a reason."

"Like decorating the cake?"

I laughed, feeling a warm glow as I felt her body close to mine. Somehow I knew our meeting was meant to be. □

AMANDA had been dreading this visit for weeks. Some mindless chatter might have helped, but Jonathan was concentrating on the stream of Sunday drivers who had invaded the country roads. Robbie was sitting in the back of the car engrossed in a book.

She didn't suppose for one moment that it was going to be any easier for Ben and Vera Appleby. In fact, it would be more difficult.

They were the ones who had seen their beautiful young daughter fall in love with Jonathan. They were the ones who had rejoiced in the birth of their first grandchild.

Now, four years after Maria's death, they were the ones who had to meet Amanda. The woman Jonathan had chosen to take their daughter's place.

"Here we are then," Jonathan announced.

"There's Grandad!" Robbie cried excitedly.

Amanda couldn't say a word — she could barely swallow.

Jonathan looked into her pale, anxious face.

"They'll love you," he said softly.

She knew he was only being his usual kind self, but how could they love her? How could they do anything but resent her?

As soon as they were out of the car, Robbie flew straight to his grandfather, and then Mrs Appleby came out.

There were hugs and kisses for Robbie, slaps on the back and kisses for Jonathan, and then Ben and Vera Appleby inched closer together.

GETTING TO KNOW YOU

"This is Amanda," Jonathan said proudly. "Amanda — Ben and Vera."

Amanda extended a trembling hand.

"I'm very pleased to meet you, Mrs Appleby. Mr Appleby. It's good of you to invite me."

The silence that met her words made Amanda long to run back to the car.

"It's good to meet you, too," Ben Appleby said at last.

"You're very welcome, Amanda." Vera forced a smile.

Jonathan was frowning slightly, Amanda noticed, but Robbie was unaware of any tension in the air.

"I'm thirsty, Gran," he said. "And I could probably manage some cake."

Thank heavens for children, Amanda thought, as she heard Vera Appleby's relieved laugh.

"Let's go and see what we can find, young man."

THE afternoon went from bad to worse as the silences grew longer. Amanda hoped that Jonathan would say something to clear the air, but he didn't. To be fair, though, what could he say?

Should she have visited the Applebys before she and Jonathan decided to marry? Perhaps she should have given them more time to accept the situation, instead of arriving once the date for their wedding had been set.

Jonathan had invited her along with him and Robbie many times, but Amanda had invented excuses until she could put it off no longer.

"Come and help me find something for tea, Robbie," Vera Appleby said. Robbie didn't need asking twice.

"Can I help?" Amanda asked.

The suggestion surprised Vera.

"Good heavens, no," she said.

Amanda watched them go, feeling embarrassed. Clearly, she wasn't welcome in the kitchen.

by
SHIRLEY
WORRALL

Tea was a demonstration of Vera Appleby's considerable cooking skills. Nothing on the table had come from a shop.

"You've been very busy," Amanda remarked.

"I enjoy cooking," was the stilted response.

"So do I," Amanda said lightly, "but I'm not very good at it. Certainly not as good as Maria was."

There! Maria's name had been mentioned. Amanda wished she hadn't been the one to do it, but something had had to be said.

Unfortunately it did nothing for the atmosphere. Jonathan looked surprised and Vera and Ben Appleby looked highly uncomfortable.

"You are a good cook," Robbie declared. "Don't you remember that treacle toffee we made for bonfire night?"

Amanda could have hugged Robbie. He was such a happy child, and so easy to love. They'd become firm friends from day one.

"That was good," she agreed, smiling at him. "But I couldn't have done it without your help."

Amanda didn't say another word during the meal. She felt awful. She felt as if she'd let Jonathan down, but half of her knew that the Applebys weren't making things any easier.

WHEN they'd finished, Amanda insisted on helping with the washing-up. The day was ruined anyway, and she hoped that if she could convince them she could use a tea towel, they might think of her as a normal human being and not just an unwelcome guest.

Drying the paper-thin bone china, Amanda wished she hadn't bothered. They didn't exchange a single word, and the only sound was the nervous hammering of Amanda's heart.

Finally, her nerves in shreds, Amanda threw down her tea towel. "Look, Mrs Appleby," she said in exasperation, "this is ridiculous. I know it's not easy for you, watching me step into your daughter's shoes, but believe me, it's not very easy for me either.

"We don't count, though, do we? You're Robbie's grandmother and I'm soon to be his stepmother. As such we'll be seeing a lot of each other in the future and we have to learn to get along — if only for his sake!"

Mrs Appleby's hands were suspended above the sink. Then, taking Amanda completely by surprise, she put those soapy hands on Amanda's shoulders and laughed. It was an odd laugh, a genuine laugh, but one that brought tears to her eyes.

"My dear girl," she said in amazement, "Ben and I have been looking forward to this visit for ages."

Amanda stared at her in disbelief.

"Nothing will bring Maria back," Mrs Appleby said quietly, "but she left us with a grandson. Do you think we want him to be unhappy? And Jonathan is just as precious to us. Do you think we want to see him unhappy?"

"Well — no," Amanda murmured. "Of course not."

"Long before Jonathan told us about you," Mrs Appleby confided, "we noticed a change in him. It was as if a ray of sunshine had sought him out. We knew he'd found someone special, and it was a joy to see him happy again."

"But today has been awful," Amanda said.

"Terrible," Mrs Appleby agreed. "You see — well, we'd been looking forward to meeting you for so long. We've heard nothing but how wonderful you are from Robbie. And then you seemed — reluctant to visit."

"I thought it might be awkward," Amanda explained, flushing with guilt.

"We thought perhaps you might want to make changes," Mrs Appleby admitted. "That perhaps you wouldn't want Robbie visiting so often, or want us visiting him."

"Of course not!" Amanda was horrified. "You're his grandparents and he loves you both dearly."

"And then, when Jonathan introduced us as Ben and Vera, you called us Mr and Mrs Appleby."

"I didn't want to be forward." Amanda groaned.

Vera chuckled. "And I thought you were putting us in our place!"

"Vera, I'm so sorry."

IT'S not your fault, Amanda. Come and look at this."

Vera walked over to a cupboard and opened a couple of cake tins. In one was a burnt fruit cake, and in the other were the broken remnants of a sponge.

"I wanted everything just so. To impress you," Vera explained with a rueful smile. "No wonder you felt ill at ease."

She gave Amanda's arm a gentle squeeze. "Let's start again, shall we?"

Smiling, Amanda nodded. "I think we should."

As they finished washing the dishes, they talked. Then they carried a tray into the garden and joined the others.

Amanda handed Ben a cup of tea. "There you are, Ben."

"And I was just thinking that Mr Appleby made me sound quite distinguished," he teased. "Thank you, Amanda," he added warmly.

Ben and Vera sat in folding chairs, and Amanda sat next to Jonathan on an old wooden seat. Robbie, having polished off four biscuits and a glass of lemonade, went in search of buried treasure at the bottom of the garden.

Everyone was trying to talk at once, and Jonathan's arm went around Amanda's shoulders as he spoke of their wedding plans. But Amanda wasn't listening.

It had taken this visit, a visit she had dreaded for so long, to make her feel at peace with herself. At the back of her mind had lurked the knowledge that she had found her happiness in someone else's tragedy. Now she knew how foolish that was.

She couldn't alter the past for these people — no-one could. But she could bring some happiness to their future. And she couldn't ask for more than that. □

MARJORY TOWERS sat down in an easy chair and rubbed her eyes with the back of her hand before reading the letter again. Auntie Else in hospital!

Elsie White, as she was then, had lived next door when Marjory was born. The teenager had adored the baby girl, and spent all the time with her she could. Marjory had been a ten-year-old bridesmaid at Elsie's wedding, and godmother to her daughter Katy, who had written the letter.

The friendship had lasted all their lives, and Katy's letter was wet with tears when Marjory laid it aside.

She must go to the hospital, and there was a bus in half an hour. That didn't give her time to get to the shops, so what could she take her friend?

Her odds and ends drawer produced nothing inspiring — talcum powder, a few cakes of

by MARY LEDGWAY

oap, the odd handkerchief. She wanted something more personal for Auntie Else. The old pet name had stuck.

Her eyes fell on the plant her daughter Anne had bought before she and the family had returned to Canada. But she couldn't part with that.

"Watch it grow and think of us," Anne had said. Marjory didn't know its name, but the leaves were dark green and glossy. Three perfectly formed flowers, miniature roses, Marjory decided, were just beginning to open out. The scent wafted through the room.

Marjory's thoughts went back to when Auntie Else was collecting toys for a children's home, many years before. She'd offered her old, broken ones and Auntie Else had shaken her head.

"No, love. Giving doesn't mean just parting with things you no longer want. It means giving something that you care about, that will give pleasure to those who receive."

Reluctantly, Marjory had parted with a favourite doll, her tea-set and a spinning top. Now, looking at the plant, she smiled. Anne would understand.

GIFT OF LOVE

Katy Baines, sitting beside her mother's bed, exclaimed with delight when she saw the plant.

"Look, Mother! See what Marjory's brought you."

She held the plant close to her, and the old lady smiled.

"I can't quite make out the flowers — but the smell is lovely. Put it on the locker near me. Thanks, Marjory. I knew you'd come." She held out a frail hand. Soon her eyes closed, and Marjory looked across at Katy.

"Sister says I can take her home in a day or two. I can manage, and the district nurse will come in." She smoothed her mother's hair. "She'll be happier at home."

TWO months later, Katy Baines lifted up the plant and looked at it tenderly. It had six flowers now, and had given so much pleasure to her mother. The perfume from the wide-open blooms had been a constant joy.

Now Mother's bed was empty. Katy carried the plant into the living-room and stood it on the wide window-sill. It seemed to bring her mother nearer.

That day the district nurse who had attended her mother knocked on the door. Katy and Judy Atkins had become friendly during those harrowing weeks, and Katy smiled with pleasure when she saw the young nurse.

"Judy! How nice. Come in."

"Well, you did say if I was in the district you would always put the kettle on." Judy laughed. "My next case is near here, so I've brought a sandwich and invited myself."

The tea Katy made was very welcome.

"I've just been at that new girl's home," Judy said when she laid down her empty beaker. "You know, Sheila Davison. They've moved into one of the new houses."

"Hasn't she just had a baby?" Katy asked.

"Yes, a little boy, Leigh. About two weeks since, but she's finding it tough going, poor lass.

"The baby is a real handful, cries on and off most of the time, and I think her husband is working long hours, and so can't do much to get the house straight. Pity she hasn't any neighbours."

"Do you think she'd like me to call?" Katy asked. "I've time on my hands."

"I'm sure she would." Judy smiled. Her little ruse had worked.

Later that afternoon, Katy looked round for something to take to Sheila. The baking was sadly depleted, and the flowers in the garden were not yet at their best.

She touched the plant. It had helped her mother — "It comforts me," she would say.

Perhaps the plant would bring pleasure to a young mother just starting out. Marjory would understand.

Sheila Davison stared when she opened the door and found Katy standing there.

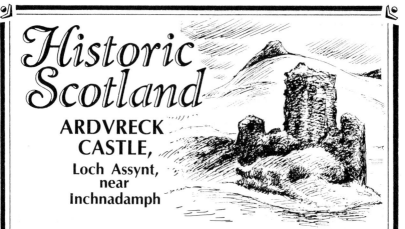

Historic Scotland

ARDVRECK CASTLE,
Loch Assynt, near Inchnadamph

ARDVRECK, a late 15th century castle standing on a rocky promontory of lovely Loch Assynt in Sutherland, is but a shell of what it once was. In its heyday it was the ancestral home of the Macleods of Assynt, associated with the Clan Graham.

In its history, however, Ardvreck will always be linked with a Graham who was not a Macleod of Assynt. This was James Graham, Marquis of Montrose.

James Graham had a remarkable and romantic career, but eventually his military successes ended at the Battle of Carbisdale in 1650, after which he fled to the North-west Highlands, hoping to re-organise his forces.

He found refuge in Ardvreck Castle, but it is said that his presence was betrayed by the Laird for the reward of £20,000 offered for his capture.

The Marquis was then taken south as a prisoner, and although he very nearly escaped when held overnight at Castle of Grange, Monifieth (when Lady Grange boldly helped him in his bid for freedom), he was eventually brought to trial and executed at Edinburgh.

The betrayal of Montrose did not remain a secret for long, and the ruined state of Ardvreck tells its own tale, for Montrose was highly thought of as a leader of men. The strange, obelisk-like mountains of Sutherland form an impressive setting for this historic episode in Scottish history.

"Hello, you must be Sheila. I'm Katy Baines from across the way. I'm sorry I haven't called earlier, but my mother was ill. I thought you might like this, a little housewarming present."

"Oh, it's beautiful! Won't you come in?"

As Katy followed her in, the sound of the baby's crying grew worse.

Katy stood over the carrycot.

"What a lovely baby!"

"He is when he's not crying." Sheila sighed. "Which isn't often."

"May I?" Katy picked the red-faced infant up. With plenty of experience, she rocked the child over her shoulder.

Gradually the sobbing grew less, and Katy, still with the baby in her arms, sat in a basket chair and smiled at the young mother.

"It will soon pass. Another couple of weeks and you'll be laughing about it."

"My mother was going to help, but — well, we had to move up here, and I don't know anybody."

"You will, once you start getting about."

Sheila, glad to have someone to talk to, made beakers of coffee, and Katy asked her about her parents and let the girl talk her troubles through.

"I'm sorry, I'm talking too much," Sheila said suddenly. "You did say your mother had been ill . . ."

"Not any more. But I had her for many years, and we were very close. I'm grateful for that.

"Look, Sheila." Katy laid Leigh back in his carrycot. "When you get things sorted out and you feel like a change, if you and your husband want to go out for an hour or two one evening, I could baby-sit. He'd be quite safe."

"Oh, would you? That would be lovely, if Sid is ever home early enough to go." But she smiled, and there was no sting in her words.

"He will be," Katy told her. "A new job always takes some getting used to."

A nice girl, she thought, as she walked home. Perhaps she could wheel little Leigh down to the shops or round the park some time, and give the young mother a bit of time to herself.

Back in the house, Sheila was looking at the plant. She found a little cloth and stood the plant in the middle of the table.

"It alters the whole room," she told herself. She looked down at her jeans, glanced at the sleeping baby, and dashed upstairs.

She slipped on a clean linen dress, added a touch of make-up and brushed her hair. When Leigh did wake up again, it didn't seem half as bad.

A FEW weeks later her husband, Sid, opened the morning paper and gave a cry of dismay.

"Oh, no! May the twenty-fourth! Dennis Franklin retires today. I meant to get him a little present."

"I thought you all clubbed together —"

"We did, but he was so good to me when I was up here on my own looking for somewhere for us to live. I thought I'd get him just some small thing for his new bungalow."

"Oh, well. It's too late now. Wouldn't be the same later."

Sheila looked at the plant. She had snipped off the lower, faded flowers, but more had taken their place and it was beautiful. Sid was right, Dennis had been good to them.

"Would you like to take this?" she offered.

"Sheila, love! I couldn't. You love that plant."

"I do, but I think it's worked its magic for us. Leigh has settled down, and we've got a fair bit done to the house. We've made friends, and I've got to know some young mothers at the clinic. Let's pass it on. Katy would understand."

Dennis Franklin drove up to his new bungalow with mixed feelings. His town flat had been just what he wanted, but now he had retired it was too expensive.

Besides, he had always promised himself a place in the country, and this was as close as he could get.

Now, as he stepped for the first time into the living-room, he felt slightly depressed. It looked so unlived in.

It was after tea when he remembered the plant, placed so carefully in the back of his car. He brought it in and stood it on the sideboard. The room seemed to come to life straightaway, and the scent!

A nice lad, that Sid Davison. He'd have to ask him and that pretty wife of his over one day.

It took Dennis quite a while to settle in. He couldn't get used to a routine not ruled by an office clock, but gradually he began to enjoy his new life.

The rest of the things from his flat had arrived, and the small garden was beginning to show a bit of colour. Inside, he tended the plant carefully and it rewarded him with still more blooms.

He spent a long time sitting by his window. Gradually he came to know his neighbours, but shy as he was, he didn't make any effort to speak to them. Until the day he saw a doctor and a nurse coming out of the small bungalow opposite.

That was where that nice, jolly-looking lady lived. Come to think of it, he hadn't seen her for a couple of days. She always walked down to collect her paper and a small bag of shopping.

He didn't even know her name. But suddenly restless, he walked down to the post office for his pension. Usually he left it two weeks, but today it was a good excuse to get out.

The post office was small and friendly. Dennis was at the back of the short queue when a lady from the front called out, "Anyone heard how Marjory Towers is?"

"Yes, nothing broken, just a sprain. Soon be fit."

"Good," the first lady replied. "She's a nice little body."

There was a murmur of agreement, and then Dennis was at the counter.

He was thoughtful as he walked back. Marjory Towers must be his opposite neighbour. "A nice little body." That was a good description.

Back inside, he looked at the plant. The room wouldn't look quite the same without it, but he was going to the garden centre to ask for advice on his small plot. He could get another plant for the house at the same time.

Carefully, if clumsily, he wrapped the plant pot and, before his courage failed him, went and knocked on Marjory's door.

COME in," a voice called.

Dennis opened the door an inch or two.

"You don't know me," he said, "but I'm from across the road. I heard you weren't well."

Marjory chuckled. "Of course I know you. Been watching you coming and going for weeks. Come on in and close the door."

Dennis walked rather nervously. Marjory lay on the settee, her ankle bandaged and a smile on her face.

"I'm perfectly well, it's just my ankle. Silly thing to do, twist it when I was getting off the bus. Never mind, could be worse. Isn't that plant rather heavy?" she added, her eyes twinkling.

Dennis flushed.

"I . . . well, I thought you might like it."

"I would — very much. It's lovely. Put it on that little stool there. It's very kind of you," she added.

"Can I get you anything? A cup of tea?"

"Everybody that comes in makes me tea! Now if you look in that cupboard, there's a wee drop of sherry left from Christmas. Now you've plucked up courage to speak to me, we'll drink to your new home."

As she lifted the glass, though, her eyes were serious.

"I do hope you'll be happy here. I hated it at first, but now I wouldn't live anywhere else."

By the time Dennis left, they knew quite a bit about each other. Walking back across the road, Dennis decided that on his next visit he would offer to take her for a run. There were many places nearby he would like to see, but it wasn't much fun without someone to share it . . .

Left alone, Marjory looked at the plant. She could have sworn it was the same type she'd taken to Auntie Else, but of course this was much bigger, stronger.

It was really beautiful, but when she removed the wrappings she exclaimed in dismay as she saw the small plant pot with the roots beginning to escape through the bottom.

"You need re-potting, my friend," she told it. "Easy to see our friend Dennis is no gardener."

Ignoring doctor's orders, she hobbled through to the kitchen and put newspaper on the draining board. It was a bit harder getting a bigger pot from the shed, but she managed.

Carefully she tapped the plant until the soil loosened, then she tipped it gently on to the newspaper. Suddenly her hands stilled.

Hardly believing her eyes, she picked up a piece of chipped blue pottery.

The same broken saucer she had put in the bottom of the pot when she had repotted the small plant Anne had bought her! Somehow, the plant she had given Auntie Else had found its way back to her.

Cast your bread upon the waters, she thought. My, but you've grown into a beauty. Wherever you've been you've been well looked after. What a pity you can't talk.

But I know one thing — now you're back at home, you're here to stay.

Her heart full of memories, she washed the broken bits of blue pottery and put them in the larger plant-pot. A labour of love. □

I'M the early riser in our family. I like that extra hour alone, browsing through the paper and gathering my thoughts for the day ahead.

That day there was a lot of information about the Festival, and who was appearing in the city. Edinburgh was crammed, as always in August.

by
GILLIAN
FRASER

Any Dream Will Do

My eye was drawn to a well-loved name.

What wonderful memories the name of Raymond Courtenay recalled. His shows had always carried me off to a world of romance. Of course, we were both young and carefree in those days, dreams much more fun than reality . . .

"Mum, you haven't laid the breakfast yet."

And of course, in those days, we didn't have Clare.

"Sorry, love," I said to my daughter. "I was just . . ."

"Another of your dreamy moments, I suppose?"

My habit of drifting away from real life was looked upon with tolerant amusement by the family.

"What are you dreaming about this time?" Clare asked.

"Not what, who. A name in the paper, someone from the past I liked very much."

I floated round the table on a wave of reminiscence, setting four places.

"His name's Raymond Courtenay. He was at his height about fifteen years ago, in romantic stage musicals. So handsome and debonair, a real heart-throb. His career faded for while, till musicals became popular again."

"So he must be quite old by now?"

"Old indeed, Clare Ritchie! He's about ten years older than me, and I'm, well, still quite young at thirty-nine."

"Nearly forty, Mum!" Clare reminded.

"Oh, you are cruel." I laughed.

"I just don't understand why women are so worried about mentioning their ages." (Clare was twelve.)

"When you reach my age, you'll find out," I warned. "Is the table laid to your satisfaction?"

"Yes, but why d'you always lay it the same way?"

"Do I?"

"Dad's place first, then mine and Peter's, and your own last."

"To tell you the truth I've never thought about it."

P 52 ▶

CROFT, SIDINISH, NORTH UIST

*T*HE *Outer Hebrides form a magical chain of islands in the Atlantic off Britain's western shores. The large island of Lewis and Harris leads down to North Uist, Benbecula and South Uist, with such islands as Eriskay and Barra forming the tail. On a sunny day in mid-summer, it's difficult to imagine a more enchanting scene than the gleaming waters of the hundreds of lochans with wild flowers in full bloom.*

CROFT, SIDINISH, NORTH UIST : J CAMPBELL KERR

But I started to think about it, because that unconscious habit was highly significant. When had I stopped being me? Nowadays I seemed to be Peter's Mum, Clare's Mum, Martin's wife, chief cook and bottle washer — never myself.

And on the rare occasions when I did sneak time for myself, what did they say? "Mum's dreaming again."

Seeing Raymond Courtenay's name had only added to my vulnerability. He was a reminder of my youth, when life was for living, with no responsibilities.

BY the time everyone had arrived for breakfast, I was still in a faraway mood, and had to be nudged by Peter.

"Pass the butter, please, Mum."

"Sorry, dear."

In reaching for it, I almost knocked over the milk jug.

"You're dreaming again!" Peter groaned.

"And I know who Mum's dreaming about," Clare said smugly.

"Who?" asked Peter with interest.

Martin, I noticed, was still buried in his paper.

I glanced round the table, and hesitated. I shouldn't be looking back over my shoulder at the past. Yet there was comfort in the telling . . .

"Raymond Courtenay!" scorned my ten-year-old. "Who'd want a name like that?"

"It looks good on the posters, Peter. He's here with a revival of 'My Only Love' before the show goes down to London.

"Your dad and I went to see the original production, and we enjoyed it so much.

"Of course, we were courting at the time, which made it all the more romantic. In fact, your dad got so carried away that he proposed to me during the performance!"

The children's eyes gazed at Martin.

"Is that true, Dad?"

Martin appeared from behind the newspaper. "Is what true?"

"That you proposed to Mum in the Playhouse during a show?"

"Yes, I did."

"What did you say?" Clare asked eagerly.

"Will you marry me?"

"Oh, Dad, I know! I mean the words in between."

"The sloppy ones," Peter added helpfully.

"I can't remember. It's a long time ago."

"I'll bet Mum remembers," Peter suggested.

"Yes, I do, but it's my secret. I'm not telling."

The children laughed, and Martin smiled, retreating once more behind his paper.

Was Martin teasing? Did he remember? Last year I'd have known for sure. But now I wasn't at all confident about him — about our marriage.

He blamed the lack of those little romantic touches on the recession. He was struggling desperately to keep the business going, to the exclusion of everything else, including me.

Clare and Peter left for school. Martin was about to leave for work.

"Final meeting with the developers today," he reminded me. "Wish me luck."

"You'll get the contract, I'm sure. You've worked so hard for it, Martin."

"Yes, but we've had some disappointments lately. I'm not raising

P 56 ▶

53

LLANGOLLEN CANAL : J CAMPBELL KERR

my hopes too high." Martin gave me a brief peck on the cheek. "See you this evening."

That was that. The morning rush was over, the debris of breakfast strewn across the table, the washing machine needing filled . . .

It was a glorious day. Would any of the family care if the dishes weren't done? I certainly didn't.

TEN minutes later I was on the bus heading for the West End. With the Festival in full swing, I crossed Princes Street and made for the Grassmarket, trying to avoid the crowds, and then joined the throng of tourists making their way up to the Castle.

I hadn't been up there for years, and had quite forgotten how wonderful the view was. I was leaning on the parapet, deep in my own thoughts, and hardly noticed the man standing next to me until he spoke.

"Marvellous view, isn't it?"

Usually I'm rather shy of strangers, but his pleasant voice, and my need to talk to someone, prompted me to reply.

"Yes. I never tire of it, and I've lived in Edinburgh all of my life."

"I hope you don't mind me talking to you like this?" he asked politely.

"No, of course not."

He sighed. "Such a pity that these days, one can't talk to a stranger without fear of ulterior motives."

"Not from me, I assure you."

He smiled his thanks. "This is my favourite view, and sharing it with someone makes me feel I belong." He added, sadly, I thought, "We all have to belong to someone, or something, don't we?"

"I'd like to come up here more often, but my work keeps me in London most of the time." He hesitated, and lifted the camera that was slung round his neck. "Would you mind taking my photograph? I'm on my own, with no-one to capture me for the family album."

"Not at all." I smiled, taking his camera.

LLANGOLLEN CANAL

SITUATED in Clwyd, Llangollen is well-known for its international annual music festival. The town, on the banks of the Dee, is surrounded by beautiful countryside. One of the local sights is the 14th-century bridge over the Dee's rapids. The Ellesmere Canal is carried over the Dee by an aquaduct.

◀ over

Framed in the viewfinder, and facing me, I recognised him immediately. After fifteen years, his hair was greyer, but apart from that, there seemed little difference.

After my initial shock, I managed a smile as I pressed the shutter.

"I hope the photo comes out all right. I'm rather nervous. It's not every day I'm asked to photograph the famous Raymond Courtenay."

Just for a moment, I had the dreadful feeling that I might have made a mistake, but then he smiled warmly.

"I've been wondering if anyone would recognise me after all these years."

"I've been a fan of yours for so long, I'd know you anywhere," I blurted out, and then kicked myself. "I'm sorry. I hope you don't mind . . . ?"

"I was the one who talked to you, remember? Besides, being recognised goes with the job. The time to start worrying is when it stops!"

"That's very kind of you, Mr Courtenay," I stammered.

"I'm the one who should be grateful to you. Have you been to the show yet?"

"I'm afraid not. My husband and I saw the original run of 'My Only Love,' back in our courting days. In fact, Martin proposed to me during the finale! So you see, we've a lot to thank you for."

He was leaning back on the parapet, interested, smiling.

"Why haven't we heard of you for a while?" I asked.

"My wife died two years ago. That's when I started my self-imposed exile from work. But it was the wrong thing for me to do, left me too much time for self-pity.

"When the revival of 'My Only Love' came up, I jumped at it. Nothing quite like work to ease the pain." His eyes were shadowed.

"It can't be an easy rôle," I said thoughtfully. "It's such a light, happy show . . ."

"That's the actor's problem, though," Raymond Courtenay said. "He's never sure who he is. You're lucky just being yourself!"

I hesitated. Dare I? Should I? But I might never have the chance again . . .

"I feel rather embarrassed, asking for your autograph at my age, but would you mind?" I asked, searching in my handbag for some paper.

"Of course not. What's your name?"

"Maureen Ritchie."

"What shall I say?" He frowned, then wrote with a flourish.

Thanks for remembering, Maureen. Best wishes, Raymond Courtenay.

"I mean it," he said, watching as I read the message. "Your recognising me has helped to restore my faith in human nature. An actor's ego, you see. I've always liked to be in the limelight!"

He flashed me a wry smile. "I hope I haven't bored you with my problems, but you seem such a sympathetic person."

"I don't mind at all."

"Then you won't be resigning from my Fan Club?"

"Hadn't thought of it!" I laughed.

"Good to know that someone still loves me." But his eyes remained sad.

"If you'll excuse me, I must go now. I've enjoyed talking to you. Goodbye, Mrs Ritchie."

"Goodbye, Mr Courtenay."

I watched him walk away down the hill, my mind in turmoil. It had all been so unexpected, and the worst of it was that I recognised the loneliness he felt. *I* was lonely.

Why was it that I could chat so easily to a stranger, and couldn't talk to my husband about anything that mattered? As I glanced down at the city I loved, I thought back to the girl Martin had proposed to.

Edinburgh was such an exciting place to be when I was young, that I'd never wanted to live anywhere else. I'd loved my job as a city guide, until Martin came along, and then I settled happily enough for domestic contentment.

But was I happy any more? Martin was still central to my life — at least, I wanted him to be. Did he still want that, too? One thing was for sure — we couldn't go on as things were for much longer.

I WENT home on the bus. It seemed terribly quiet without Clare and Peter. They were staying with grandparents overnight.

Would Martin be remotely interested in my meeting with Raymond Courtenay? Should I even bother him with such a triviality, while the contract decision was on his mind?

I heard the familiar crunch of his feet on the gravel, and went to open the door.

He burst into the hall, laughing — when had I last heard his laugh? He picked me up and kissed me.

"Put your coat on, darling! We're going out to celebrate."

"You've won the contract?"

"Exactly the opposite."

"Put me down, Martin," I ordered. "Then why the celebration?"

NEIDPATH CASTLE

*O*NE *of reputedly eighty peel-towers in Peebles-shire, Neidpath Castle is now unoccupied but kept in good condition by its owner, the Earl of Wemyss and March. It was a stronghold of the Frasers until the 14th century, when it came by marriage to Hay of Yester. The castle is only a mile from Peebles, and popular with holiday-makers.*

NEIDPATH CASTLE : J CAMPBELL KERR

"Relief, sweetheart. Things have been so tense with that decision looming, and I haven't been able to think about anything else. I've barely said a word to you or the children.

"Getting my priorities right again, that's what I want to celebrate."

"I'll need a few minutes to make myself look beautiful."

"That shouldn't take long." Martin grinned.

"Flatterer!" I said, already on my way upstairs.

The meal at the Italian trattoria left us in mellow mood.

"I'm sorry you missed out on the contract, Martin."

"I'm not, love. It would have stretched me too far. Tendering for a contract that size was rather ambitious.

"At the moment I want to concentrate on the contract I've been neglecting lately . . . our marriage contract. We're just in nice time for a special treat."

"What?"

"A visit to the theatre. Two seats, centre stalls, for this evening's performance of 'My Only Love'."

Tears of joy filled my eyes.

"Oh, Martin!"

He took my hand in his. "That show was very special for both of us."

"Was it? This morning you told the kids you couldn't remember what you said to me."

"Of course I remembered, but I wasn't going to confess in front of them. They'd have laughed their heads off!"

He grinned. "I might even give a repeat performance this evening. When the finale comes up I'll whisper, 'Maureen, you'll always be my only love. Will you marry me?' "

"Only this time," I suggested, "don't spoil my concentration while Raymond's singing."

"So you're on first name terms now?"

"Just since I met him," I said.

Martin's eyes widened with surprise.

"Tell me more."

I fished in my bag for the autograph, and told him all about it.

"I suppose you fancy him even more now?" Martin said, with a straight face.

"No! Talking to him made me realise. He's just like anyone else struggling to make a living, and lonely since his wife died. He said I was lucky to have someone to love."

"And are you?" Martin said, putting an arm round her shoulder.

"Yes, darling. What a pity it took Raymond Courtenay to make me see just how lucky I am."

"Are you sure you won't fall for him all over again?" Martin teased.

I laughed, and kissed him lingeringly.

"No. Dreams are all right, but they don't last very long. I'd rather spend a lifetime of reality with you . . ."

"My only love," he said softly. □

FLOWERS
FOR THE ANIMALS

WHEN people go in their garden,
They like to see the flowers,
But there's something very special
About the blooms in ours.

There are bells for the hare,
And gloves for the fox,
Lilies for the tiger grow,
Close beside the phlox.

We've got willow for the pussy,
And roses for the dog,
And in a sheltered corner,
Well past the froggy bog,
If you're still and quiet,
You'll hear muted thunderclaps,
That is where the dragons go,
To test their precious snaps.

I don't know when the animals
Come to pick their flowers,
Is it in the dewy dawn,
Or in the twilight hours?

Dad says I'll never see them,
Because they're all too shy,
But I hope to prove him wrong
Someday — by and by!

— Linda Leigh.

61

The Day I Was Wicked!

WHAT in the world had got into me that day? Normally I'm a sensible, law-abiding woman. But on that particular Monday morning I did the stupidest thing imaginable. I'm not a youngster either, I'm nearly sixty.

Mind you, my head was just clearing from a cold, and the winter had been a long and dreary one.

I'd had no sympathy from my husband, Ian. He hadn't even noticed my sniffs and sneezes. I had stayed on my feet doing all the housework, cooking and shopping, and to be honest, I have never been much good as a martyr.

On that Monday morning, Ian had gazed out of the kitchen window as he munched his toast. Five minutes more and he would be dashing off to work.

"Lucky you!" he said. "What a glorious morning!"

The view from our window was of low-lying hills. A patchwork of green and gold fields lies criss-crossed with hedges and trees. I knew that his eyes were to the hills, but mine couldn't see past the crumbstrewn tablecloth and all the clutter of the kitchen.

I lifted my coffee cup and went to the window, forcing myself to shake off my gloom and look outwards. Something did catch my eye.

by JENNIE BOLWELL

In the field behind our bungalow, there was a brown pony. We shared a fellow feeling, that pony and I. Alone in his field, he seldom had a visitor.

Now that my family had grown and gone, once Ian went off to work, I spent most of the day on my own. Ian and I had moved here quite recently, so I knew very few people.

So I made friends with the pony. I carried out to him my brussels sprouts peelings and the odd carrot or two. I called him Beauty, although he wasn't. He was short legged, with a rather large beam-end.

He was there now, stamping his feet on the ground and tossing that shaggy mane.

"A lovely summer's day," said Ian wistfully, as though he would like to swap places with me. Perhaps there was madness in the air that morning. And perhaps the pony felt it, too.

Ian drained the last drop from his cup.

"Must dash!" he said, as he always did every morning, and added something else he always said. I think it started as a directive to the children. He gave me a quick kiss and said — "Be good!"

Be good! Most mornings I was so used to it, I didn't even hear it. But this morning I did. And the words rankled!

I had been good for far too long. If a good fairy had given me just one wish, I would have said, "Let me be wicked!" But what chance has a sensible, law-abiding sixty-ish woman of that?

I turned my back on the crumbs and disorder of the kitchen. After all, I had all day to attend to that. I picked up the bowl with last night's vegetable scraps, put in an apple for good measure, and I sauntered down to the gate of the field.

"Beauty!" I called.

There was an answering whinny, then the sound of his hoof-beats as he galloped to meet me. I let myself in, and tied the gate behind me.

I felt a rush of love for him. Perhaps I was tricked into thinking that he felt the same for me. As I stroked his forehead, the strong horsy smell of him triggered off a childhood memory.

When I was a little girl, there used to be an old retired pit pony who ended his days in the glebe next to the church where my grandfather was minister. Hidden from view from all windows, I used to make-believe I was a dare-devil circus rider.

I would climb on his back and ride him bare-back round the field. Most of the thrill came from the fact that I knew it was forbidden, but, oh, the exhilaration of it!

That was the moment when mad desire took hold of me.

"Beauty!" I whispered into his ear. "Would you let me try? Just for a little while?"

He let me mount without much trouble. It wasn't till I was up there that it seemed to dawn on him what was happening.

He didn't wait for any slap on the rump, he just took off.

"Whoa! Stop, Beauty! Stop!"

This wasn't an old, done horse. This morning Beauty was young and spirited.

"Whoaaah!" I screamed in his ear, and clung on like grim death. He didn't try to throw me, and he did seem to slow down a bit. Perhaps if I could steer him towards the gate, I thought, he might stop beside the discarded vegetable bowl which he knew so well.

I tugged at his mane. He did turn towards the gate. I gripped him firmly with my knees.

"Good boy!" I said, and was just congratulating myself when suddenly I realised that he had no intention of stopping at the gate. He was going to jump it!

I entwined my hands in the tangle of his mane, shut my eyes tight, and said a quick prayer.

"Ooooo-aaah!"

I couldn't believe I was still on his back and all in one piece. Once on the roadway, it became obvious that he knew where he was going. He was trotting at a fairly steady pace. However, there was no thought of my jumping off. So I tried to pretend to Beauty — and to myself — that I knew how to ride. Hadn't I watched the experts on television often enough?

We passed the post van coming in the opposite direction. It slowed down and stopped.

I caught a glimpse of the postman's face. I knew that I must look as foolish as I felt, but there was nothing I could do.

I remembered that in a field nearer the village, there was one of those big, beautiful, Clydesdale mares with her foal.

The Day I Was Wicked!

"Please, Beauty! Stop and say hello to her," I begged.

His ears twitched, but his trot remained steady.

In the field with the mare and foal, I saw a man carrying a bale of hay. He must have heard our clip-clop on the roadway, because he turned round and stared.

"Hoy!" he shouted. He began waving his arms wildly at me. He looked furiously angry, but his words were lost in the wind as we went by.

Then I saw an elderly lady pushing her shopping trolley towards the village. I had often seen her when I went out shopping. She looked such a nice person. Everyone seemed to know her and speak to her, and I had even hoped that one day I, too, might make her acquaintance.

But gone now was any hope of friendship as she stopped at the side of the road and gazed.

Alas! She would know me now for the nut-case I assuredly was. I clung to the horse with all my strength and looked back at the woman helplessly.

A S I neared the village, the fear of falling off receded and a new terror took its place. Everyone would stop and point. I would be the laughing stock of the whole countryside.

But, just at the point when that horse had almost reduced me to tears, he turned in at a wide gateway.

The farm! Of course! He had known all along where he was going. He ambled to a halt in the middle of a courtyard, and gave one of his friendly whinnies.

Once I had made quite certain that his back had stopped moving, I disentangled my fingers from his wiry mane and brought one leg up and over to meet the other, then I slithered to the ground.

The farm door opened and a plump, middle-aged woman ran out and was just in time to break my fall.

"Lord'a mercy! What in the name of all creation are you doing with Mephistopheles?"

Then she must have seen my white, shocked face, for she took command of the situation.

She shouted to someone to take care of the horse and then she put a capable arm round me and steered me towards the house.

"What you need is a good, strong cup of tea," she said.

Gratefully I sank into the biggest, softest armchair.

"I — I —" I tried desperately to think how to begin to explain, but she stopped me.

"Not till I've made the tea," she said. "I want to enjoy listening to this."

I hadn't a clue how I was going to get out of this, but it was bliss just being alive. By the time a mug of tea was put into my hand, my legs had stopped shaking and I was able to smile at her.

She sat in a chair beside me and looked so sympathetic that I began to confess it all to her. My loneliness, my peevishness towards my husband for not noticing my wretched cold, and then my terrible urge to be wicked.

"Well, I've done it now!" I finished. "No-one will have anything to do with me now."

But my new friend was laughing.

"Och! No harm's been done. Folk like a good laugh. I've known you simply as Mrs Brown of Hillside. You always looked so serious, I never thought you would be the kind of person who'd get on with me!" She laughed again. "That's just the kind of daft prank I enjoy. Let's introduce ourselves. I'm Peg Morton — just call me Peg."

"And my name is Janet," I said.

"Will you have a scone, Janet?" Peg asked. "And a little more tea?"

"Yes, please," I said, settling into the armchair.

"Mephistopheles is my daughter's pony," Peg exclaimed. "Marie's just started university and hasn't so much time to spend with him. My husband, Bob, keeps an eye on him when he takes hay up to the cattle farther up the glen."

Peg gave another chuckle.

"Wait till I tell Marie about this! I warned her it was a mistake to teach him to jump. I half expected him to arrive back here, but I never thought for a moment that he would bring a passenger with him!"

By now I was able to laugh, too. The tea had revived me, and I was enjoying the company of this cheery woman, when suddenly the door burst open and the angry man I had seen earlier came charging in.

"You won't believe it, Peg!" he roared. "I've just seen someone stealing Mephistopheles!"

His face was red with anger, and I cringed.

"No, no, Bob! You've got it all wrong," Peg said calmly. "It was Mephistopheles who was running off with Janet here. Janet, meet my husband, Bob!"

She explained, making it sound quite reasonable for a woman of my age to go bare-back riding.

"Whew!" He let out a long, low whistle. "And you're sure you're none the worse?"

I ached all over, but I smiled and said, "Oh, I'm fine!"

"Well, that's a mercy. You could have killed yourself!"

He was no sooner gone, than there was a knock at the back door, and I recognised the postman's voice. Peg went to collect the mail.

"Do you know that snooty woman who is new up at Hillside?" I heard her being asked.

"What about her?" asked Peg. "Speak up, Archie. I'm not hearing so well this morning."

"I saw her riding a horse," he said. "But she can't really be very posh."

"Oh? Why not?"

The Day I Was Wicked!

"The horse had no saddle," Archie said. "She was only wearing an old sweater and trousers — and she wasn't very good at it!" he added with disgust.

"Maybe she isn't so snooty after all," Peg said.

I could hear the laughter in her voice.

Well! I thought, if people have been avoiding me because they think me snooty, I can do something about it.

PEG had no sooner got another sip of her tea, when there was another knock. This time she ushered in the lady with the trolley who'd gazed after me.

"I want you to meet Miss Gordon," Peg said, introducing us. "Miss Gordon is the retired headmistress of our local school."

My muscles were stiffening rapidly, but I struggled respectfully to my feet and shook hands with her.

"Oh, I am so glad that everything is all right," she said. "I was worried about you."

Once more Peg did the explaining, leaving out unflattering details.

"How brave of you!" Miss Gordon burst out. "You know, that is something I have always longed to do, but I have never had the nerve." Her eyes were full of admiration.

She joined us for a cup of tea, and we chatted like friends. Later, Peg Morton drove me home.

"Tell Marie when she visits Mephistopheles to come in and have a hot drink with us," I said.

"Thanks! I will. See you soon!" she said before she drove off.

Even after a long, hot soak in the bath, my body still ached. I limped about the house, wondering how I should tell Ian about my day's adventure.

I was rehearsing my story, when suddenly, to my surprise I heard his car arriving home.

He was far too early. Could there be something wrong? I went to meet him.

Yes, he did look a bit anxious.

"Janet!" he said. "I have a confession to make."

I stood stock still.

"It was such a lovely morning this morning, I must have gone a little mad."

"Ian!" I said. "What have you done?"

"You have had such a rotten cold and you looked so unhappy this morning, that I went straight into the office and arranged to have a fortnight off.

"Then I went to the travel agent and booked a holiday in the sun for us. I'm sorry, I didn't take time to consult you. I just went ahead and did it."

I went into his arms.

"I have a confession to make too," I told him. "But mine can wait. I like the sound of yours so much better!" □

MIDSUMMER

JENNIFER GORDON was furious. She climbed up the steep bank of Cairney Knowe with determination, her mouth set firm, her brown eyes hard and unrelenting. At last she reached the top and flung herself down on the grass.

It was all over with Nigel Ward. He was out of her life for ever.

Cairney Knowe held a special place in Jennifer's heart. As a child, she'd attributed magical qualities to this mound which was only half a mile from home, on the old road that was seldom used now.

Here, she had brought her little problems and always, it seemed, she'd found some helpful solution. Even now, in the maturity of her twenty-two years, a visit here could still bring comfort. Only last week when an uneasiness had gripped Jennifer because of Nigel's surprising coolness on the telephone, she'd been soothed, telling herself that her imagination had run riot.

But there could be no solace here on this lovely summer evening. The hills and the fields were vivid in their various colours. She lay back and looked up at the clear blue sky. Around her was the sweet scent of the grass and the trees. But Jennifer was completely oblivious to all that beauty.

She felt numb now. Today's happenings had drained her, making her weak and exhausted.

Jennifer was an assistant in her father's shop, an old-established gentlemen's outfitter in this country town. Nigel had come in to buy a tie and she'd served him. A week later, he returned, and bought another.

"I saw you in the bank when I was in the other day," Jennifer said. "You've just recently arrived, haven't you?"

"Yes, I came up from London about three weeks ago," he told her. "The bank has sent me here to gain some experience before I move on to a more responsible job."

He was a very assured young man, immaculately dressed.

"It must be quite a change for you to come to this quiet place."

"Yes, I'm missing the bright lights," Nigel admitted.

He smiled, and she was immediately caught up in his charm. There was no denying his good looks with his clear-cut features, and his light-blue eyes that seemed to hold a magnetic quality.

EVENTS moved quickly after that. At Jennifer's suggestion, Nigel joined the badminton club and from there he received introductions to further activities. One evening he escorted Jennifer home and she was flattered that this sophisticated young man, who had rapidly become highly popular, should single her out

MADNESS

for special attention.

And so, as the months passed, their friendship became firmly established. Nigel would come to the Gordons for meals and there was always an open door for this stranger in their midst. He, in turn, would escort Jennifer to dances and take her out sometimes for a run to the seaside or to the latest popular restaurant in the district.

Life seemed wonderful. With two hearts beating as one, their future together seemed set and secure. They dreamed their dreams, building castles in the air. Nothing could spoil this idyllic existence.

It was like a stone being thrown into a placid pool when Nigel's promotion came. A year was such a short time to be together, and they were upset at the prospect of parting. But seventy miles wasn't at the other side of the world. Each had a car and they could laugh at the miles.

At first, they'd phoned every evening, their conversation extravagant in its intensity. Nigel came over to Jennifer's home once or twice until they

compromised by meeting halfway. Distance did not slacken the bond between them, their world was as marvellous as ever. Until that first hint, last week, that had caused Jennifer to shiver and to wonder.

by
NAN
BAXTER

69

Today, they'd met at a village that had a river running through its public park. The water was high after a storm of wind and rain. Nigel had thrown in a piece of wood and it was immediately swept away in the current.

"That'll reach the sea in half an hour," he declared, "which reminds me, I've got to get away early."

"Why?" asked Jennifer.

Strangely enough, Nigel hesitated.

"It's very important," he answered. "A fellow I know is coming with a lot of business information for me, and his time is limited."

Somehow, Jennifer sensed his explanation didn't ring true. Business on a Saturday afternoon sounded highly improbable. She looked at Nigel, searchingly, but he averted his eyes, and immediately she was suspicious.

Jennifer was still lying back in the grass and everything connected with today's meeting was so clear. She could even visualise the herring-bone pattern of Nigel's brown sports jacket.

"I've got something to tell you," Nigel started off, and by the tone of his voice Jennifer feared the worst. She waited, perplexed.

"This is going to be very difficult," continued Nigel and, immediately, Jennifer knew, without a doubt, that someone else was now the girl in his life.

"You've found another girl, haven't you?" she questioned bravely. What was the point of protracting this issue? Deliberately, she was making it easier for him and he grasped this opportunity.

"Yes," he continued. "I'm sorry, Jennifer. These things happen. Better now than later. I hope we'll still remain friends."

She didn't answer. What could she say?

"Let's go to the pub and have a drink," he suggested, and, at that, Jennifer stood up.

The blatant arrogance of the man, the conceit of him, and the cold-blooded cruelty! What did it matter to Nigel Ward that he was breaking her heart? Jennifer was digging her nails into her hands. She was too proud to let him see her cry.

"I never knew that love could die so quickly," she said, facing him.

There was no emotion in Jennifer's voice and Nigel Ward had the grace to hang his head. She walked away. Once, she stumbled and almost fell, but there was no-one to help her. Already, she was starting to face life alone.

Jennifer was sobbing now, and all her defences were down. But out of her confusion there emerged, realistically, the consolation that she'd escaped from a man of feeble character. Yet she knew her wounds wouldn't heal in a day.

PERHAPS she sobbed herself to sleep, but it was some time later that she heard the sound of bagpipes, and realised it wasn't a dream. She sat up, blinked, and looked down. There, at the side of the road was her little car, but now two others were parked beside it.

A group of young people surrounded the piper. He was playing a well-known tune and she'd danced to it often, Jennifer recalled. It seemed to her as if these people were about to dance on that triangle of grass where a farm track joined the old road. Some of them were doing the odd step or two, but they were not forming up. She watched closely and, obviously, they were having a discussion.

Someone looked up in her direction, and then a young man detached himself from the others and was coming towards her. This big, sturdy fellow was climbing swiftly.

Jennifer stood up. What in all the world was this stranger wanting with her? Then he was by her side, regarding her in a tentative sort of way.

"I hope you don't think this is very impertinent of me," he began. "I'm Mike Sutherland. We're all on our way home after an outing, but it's such a lovely night we'd like to dance an eightsome reel. But we're a girl short, and then we saw you, and wondered, if by any chance, you could fill in. What do you say?"

She hesitated.

"I can dance the eightsome reel," Jennifer divulged, "but I'm afraid . . ."

"Don't be afraid." The young man was smiling to her appealingly. "I can assure you we're quite a respectable bunch."

Jennifer was in no mood to dance, but she couldn't tell him that. No doubt he'd noticed traces of tears on her face, and was wondering, too, why she was sitting up here alone. To refuse now would be rude. Besides, a little excitement might cheer her up if only for a few minutes.

"I'll be happy to come," she said simply, and managed a smile.

"You're a real sport." Mike Sutherland's dark eyes crinkled in delight.

"What's your name?" he asked, and she told him. Then he took her hand and they ran down, like a couple of children. It was good to laugh again.

There were introductions all round. Mike's sister, Katrina, took it upon herself to tell Jennifer how such a party as this had formed. Two years ago, she explained briefly, a few of them had met and arranged that whenever possible, they should all set out together and do something of interest. Gradually, their numbers had grown. Today, they'd visited an agricultural show.

But there was little time for talk.

"Take your partners," someone called out.

"I found you, Jennifer," said Mike, bowing. "So I claim this privilege."

They danced well. The grass was rough here and there, and sometimes someone slipped. But what did that matter? Everyone was smiling, enjoying themselves to the full. Even Jennifer's pain had slightly lessened.

"That was good." Mike was complimenting her.

They all gravitated to a grassy bank to relax and then to talk. They were a kindly lot and Jennifer was not left out. They chatted freely and told Jennifer of their various jobs. Mike was a vet, Katrina a nurse in the cottage hospital while Hamish MacDonald, who played the pipes at every opportunity, was a farmer. The others had mainly country jobs, too.

"I've got the feeling," said Katrina, eyeing Jennifer, "that I've met you somewhere before."

"Perhaps in my father's shop," suggested Jennifer. "Gordon's, the gents' outfitter."

"That's it," Katrina agreed. "I remember going in to buy shirts for my father." And then she was regarding Jennifer even more intently.

"I think you might be the very person we're looking for," she said seriously. "One of the girls in our group got married recently and is off to Canada. We need a substitute to keep up our numbers. Why shouldn't it be you? You'd be most welcome."

IT was all so unexpected and wonderful, like walking from darkness into light.

"Everyone's so friendly and kind," said Jennifer, still marvelling at the sudden turn of events. "Yes, I'd love to join you." And she meant it with all her heart.

"Then I'll come and see you some day soon," promised Katrina.

But the dancing wasn't over. Mike was raising his voice.

"A quadrille," he shouted, "and then, perhaps, we'd better head home."

Jennifer danced with a forestry worker this time, but when they finished and goodbyes were being said, it was Mike Sutherland who escorted Jennifer to her car.

"I could have danced all night," declared Mike, and he was humming the tune of the song.

"Me, too," added Jennifer.

"I don't think I'll ever forget tonight." Mike was beaming. "It's fun to be a little mad at times, and this is the right time to let yourself go. Did you realise that this is Midsummer Night?"

"No, I didn't." Jennifer laughed, a little bell-like sound that was captivating. In the evening air, there came the scent of honeysuckle. It was such a heavenly night. She, too, would never forget it.

Jennifer got into her car, and everyone was waving. As she drove on, her thoughts were in complete disorder until, suddenly, with all its sickening certainty, there came the reminder of today's anguish. It would be with her for a long time, she knew.

And then, joyfully, she was recalling those new friends she'd just left, good, substantial people who would provide a shelter for her suffering.

Every day now would be a healing day and every tomorrow a day of promise, for there was a new light on her horizon. Her childhood trust in the magic of Cairney Knowe had worked again. And Jennifer smiled. □

Candytuft Magic

by JOAN M. NEWBY

EILEEN gazed with amusement at the free gift attached to her magazine. What use was a packet of candytuft seeds to her in a third-floor flat?

Her mind drifted back to the home she had sold before moving into this small, labour-saving flat on the Grenham Estate. It was the garden she remembered best. It had been the hardest wrench of all, leaving her garden behind.

Daffodils and blossom in spring, velvety roses in June, autumn's dahlias and Michaelmas daisies, the tracery of trees against a winter sky . . . the garden had been a living calendar. They had planned and cherished it together, she and Jim.

After his death, Eileen had taken great comfort in the garden. Tending living things made Jim seem closer. It was as if, wherever she went, among the flowers and trees and shrubs, she glimpsed his shadow just slightly ahead of her.

But the place was just too big. To watch it decay from neglect would break her heart. Better to sell now, she decided.

In some way, she supposed, she and Jim had poured the love they would have lavished on children on to each other and their home. Now, she had lost Jim, and her beloved garden, and it was taking her a very long time to come to terms with it.

Oh, the flat was comfortable, more economical than a rambling house, and she had made new friends. Yet she still pined for the countryside she had left.

Sometimes she gazed out at the sky and longed to take flight with the starlings.

There was one special angle from which she could glimpse a distant meadow and a cluster of trees. She came to regard it as her own personal view.

She walked across to the window now and saw the sun appear from

73

behind banks of cloud. That tempted her out. She did a few errands at the shops, then turned in the direction of the little sanctuary she had discovered.

B EHIND the estate, verging on open ground, was a small patch of garden; a winding path between grassy banks, some shrubs, one or two trees and a shabby park bench.

She had come across it on a misty autumn afternoon, and her heart had lifted at the smell of damp earth, the sight of leaves and grass. She had heard a robin chirping from a branch, and caught sight of sparrows and starlings hunting for food. Next time she went, she scattered crumbs for the birds.

From then on, she went to the garden almost every day, until she believed the birds knew she was their friend. In February she found a few snowdrops bravely blooming under a tree, and in April there were daffodils fluttering in the breeze.

Today she allowed the little garden to work its magic on her as usual. She came away refreshed in spirit, and wondered whether to plant her free seeds there. A splash of candytuft would certainly brighten it up, and it was such a pity not to give the seeds a chance to grow.

Back at the flats, she met old Mr Pennycook from downstairs.

"Is it cold out?" he asked.

"No," Eileen told him.

"I'm not sure I'll chance it. My old knees are playing up."

While he hesitated, the lift descended and Mrs Atkins from the top floor emerged.

"Have you heard there's going to be a lot of building done behind the estate?" she asked breathlessly. "They're going to put a whole lot of flats on that spare land."

"Everywhere's going to be built up the way they're going on," Mr Pennycook growled

"Well, the land's no use to anyone as it is," Mrs Atkins pointed out.

"What about the little garden?" asked Eileen.

"What garden?" asked Mr Pennycook.

"Do you mean that spot where there's an old bench?" Mrs Atkins said.

Eileen nodded.

"Oh, that will go. Part of the package. I suppose some people will object, someone objects to everything. Personally I'm all for progress — that wasteland's an eyesore."

"Can't stop these developers," muttered Mr Pennycook. "Not when there's money in it."

"I must say Joss Maybury needs some stopping," Mrs Atkins agreed. "He must own half the town by now."

Sick at heart, Eileen left them to put the world to rights, and climbed the stairs. She had heard of Joss Maybury. Who hadn't? He was a wealthy widower, head of a development company.

If he chose to fill the land behind the estate with more blocks of flats, nothing would stop him. It was only to her that the small patch of grass and shrubs was such a comfort and inspiration. The birds would soon have to seek new homes. She sighed.

That same evening, there was a paragraph in the evening paper.

A continuation of Grenham Estate, the building will be of the same high standard, and providing quality homes within easy access of shops and buses. There was a smudgy photograph of Joss Maybury.

He looked quite benevolent, Eileen thought, but any benevolence wouldn't interfere with his business acumen.

The film on TV that night was rubbish. Her thoughts kept wandering, and perhaps that was why the idea came to her.

She would go and see the all-powerful Mr Maybury, she decided. What, after all, had she to lose? There were times, she told herself, when you had to stand up and be counted, and this was one of them.

NEXT morning, after a brief visit to her garden to give her courage, Eileen caught the bus into town.

Maybury Enterprises lived in an imposing building. She took a deep breath and went in.

It took time and persistence to get past a receptionist and a secretary, but eventually Eileen was shown into Joss Maybury's inner sanctum.

He was a well-built, jovial-looking man. The photo had captured his broad smile, Eileen thought as he rose from his desk to greet her.

"Mrs Shaw? Take a seat. What can I do for you?" He settled back.

"I'm from Grenham Estate," Eileen began nervously. But as she explained her mission, her voice grew stronger. She told him what the little spread of garden had come to mean to her.

"If it's lost, it will be one more little piece of nature gone for ever," she finished. "Can't it possibly just be left alone?"

Mr Maybury had taken his glasses off, and his sea-blue eyes held a twinkle of good humour.

"Well, Mrs Shaw, I appreciate your point and I'm all in favour of conservation, but we've got to be practical.

"People badly need homes. Unlike your birds, they can't go flying off somewhere else to nest . . ."

He seemed pleased with that, but Eileen stared at him stonily.

"I'm not objecting to more homes being built," she retorted. "All I'm asking you to do is to preserve a small patch of garden for the benefit of everyone."

"Who's everyone? Why haven't you brought me a petition filled with signatures, if people are so anxious to have the garden preserved?

"I've got my ear to the ground, Mrs Shaw, and most of the residents on the estate don't even know that place exists. You expect me to divert an access road simply for the sake of a bit of grass and a few bushes?"

Eileen felt her colour rise. She rose to her feet.

"I understand, Mr Maybury, that in your view I'm just a silly, old-fashioned woman, out of step with today's world. Perhaps you're right. I don't fit in with the profiteering rat-race that goes on, and I never will.

"But I'd like to remind you that there's more to life than money and big business, just as there's a lot more to that bit of grass and those mouldy bushes than someone like you could possibly understand."

She reached for the packet of candytuft seeds, and slapped them down on his desk.

"I meant to sow these in that little garden to add a bit of colour. Now they'll never be planted. They'll be wasted, just as the garden you so despise will be laid to waste beneath the bulldozers.

"I'm sorry to have troubled you. Good morning, Mr Maybury."

She turned her back on him and stalked out.

And that was that, she thought, a wasted journey. Too dispirited to go window-shopping, she caught the bus back home.

A WEEK went by, then one afternoon there was a ring at the door. Eileen was astonished to find Joss Maybury standing there.

"Good afternoon, Mrs Shaw." He beamed at her. "I'm glad I've found you. May I come in for a minute?"

"Yes, of course." Bewildered, Eileen stood aside. "Please — do sit down."

He took the armchair, his blue eyes glancing appreciatively round the cosy room.

"You've made this very pleasant, Mrs Shaw." He nodded towards the row of house-plants on the window-ledge. "I see you're a wizard with those."

"One of my interests." Eileen felt awkward. "Would you like a drink?" she offered. "Tea, perhaps?"

"Not just yet," he responded. "Do sit down, I want to talk to you."

He waited while Eileen sat on the settee before going on.

"After you'd been to see me, I went out to have a look at that garden of yours."

He paused, and Eileen held her breath.

"You know, you've got something there. We're covering acres of our beautiful land with brick and concrete, and people are losing touch with their roots.

"Now, I can't save your garden. I've gone over the plans time and time again, but I'm afraid it will have to go."

Eileen gave a deep sigh.

"At least you've tried," she murmured.

"Yes, I have. But there's another idea which I'm determined to carry through.

"I've decided to build some bungalows as well as flats on that land,

Historic Scotland

TANTALLON CASTLE,
North Berwick

ROSE-COLOURED and resplendent in the morning light, Tantallon Castle faces the Bass Rock from its clifftops' eyrie, and rivals it as a feature of the North Berwick coast.

At one time, to "Ding doon" (destroy) Tantallon in popular speech meant the height of impossibility. Yet, after many sieges, it was eventually captured and dismantled by General Monk in 1651, during the Cromwellian occupation of Scotland.

At one time Tantallon was a moated castle, and with its round towers and imposing gatehouse, dating in part from the 14th century, it still carries an impregnable look. It is by no means a ragged, fragmentary ruin.

In his narrative poem, "Marmion," Sir Walter Scott ably describes this romantic stronghold of the Douglases. The passage about the hero's hair's-breadth escape on horseback over the castle drawbridge is told with great vigour and excitement.

and they'll each have a small garden. They'll be for people like you, who would love and cherish them.

"If you put your name down for one, I can guarantee you first chance of a garden bungalow. What do you think of that?" He leaned back in his chair.

Eileen felt too breathless to speak for a moment. A bungalow with a garden! There was a catch in her voice when she finally spoke.

"I think it's a wonderful plan. But I'm not sure if I could afford it."

His eyes twinkled.

"I think you could. They'll be the same price as this place."

Eileen gasped. For a moment she couldn't find words.

"With any luck, your friendly birds may find homes in your new garden," he said gently. "It won't be big, you know, just room for a little lawn, a flower-bed or two, perhaps a lilac tree . . ."

Wallflowers, forget-me-nots, roses, marigolds! Eileen felt a surge of pure happiness.

"It was the candytuft that brought it home to me," he was saying. "Gwen, my wife, used to love it, always had some in the garden. Seeing that packet of seeds brought it all back, what I've lost, without her . . ." He broke off, and they were silent for a moment.

"Anyway." He drew the candytuft seeds from his pocket, and handed them to Eileen. "Here's a pledge for the future. Now, how about that tea?"

With a light heart, Eileen went to make it. She thought about the garden where she would plant her candytuft, of the seeds she would plant, and of a more important seed — that of a new friendship. □

Romance In The Air

NOW, Mr Forder, ready for visiting, are we?" Nurse Sims asked, plumping up the pillows on Derek's bed.

Derek groaned. Nurse Sims was as brisk as ever.

"No need to feel sorry for yourself, Mr Forder. I know you don't get many visitors, but you ought to be thankful you're all in one piece after a car smash like yours."

Derek made no reply. Nurse Sims meant well, and he *knew* he should be grateful. But lying by himself in this little side-ward, the only bed vacant when they brought him in, he was beginning to feel lonely. Especially at visiting time.

Nurse Sims smoothed the counterpane and moved towards the door.

"Maybe you'll be lucky this afternoon and have someone to see you. You're new to this town, aren't you?"

Derek nodded. So new, he hadn't had time to make any friends. The chaps from his office had come to visit at first, but he couldn't blame them for drifting away. He couldn't blame his landlady either. She was kind, but busy, and it was a long bus ride from Nelson Street to the City Hospital just to see him.

Nurse Sims paused at the door.

"Takes time to get to know folk, Mr Forder. What about your mum and dad?"

Then, seeing the look on his face, she stopped abruptly.

"I see. No family, either. Never mind, I'll get one of our walking patients to drop in and cheer you up. Can't have you getting depressed, can we?"

Derek lay watching the door that never opened. Then suddenly it did.

"You the new lad here? I'm Joe Phillips. They told me you needed a visitor. New to these parts, then, are you, laddie?"

He sat down heavily on the bedside chair, his crutches on the floor beside him.

"This old leg's nearly healed. I'm going out in a few days' time. How about you? Car smash, was it?"

"The car's a write-off, they tell me." Derek nodded ruefully. "Just my luck on my first week up here."

"Well, you've certainly got VIP treatment, laddie," Joe said, looking round the little ward. "A room of your own, and all the pretty nurses to yourself, eh? Better be careful what you tell your girlfriend or she'll be getting jealous!"

Derek grinned. No use admitting to Joe that he hadn't got a girlfriend. And Nurse Sims was no catch!

"Dull for a young chap like you," Joe went on. "Still, you wait till tomorrow. Our Rosaleen'll be back from her holiday and she'll raise your spirits, you'll see."

by EILEEN ELIAS

Derek propped himself on one elbow. "Rosaleen?"

"She's the music lady," Joe said. "Every morning, ten-thirty on the dot. Sort of disc jockey. Send in your request one day and next morning it's on the air.

"Wonderful, this hospital radio is. Anything you want, she'll find and play — soul, rock, country 'n' western. Classical even, if you like that sort of thing. I tell you, we've missed her these last two weeks while she's been away."

THAT afternoon, Nurse Sims came in for Derek's request. It had taken him quite a while to choose it, and he'd lingered over his tea tray, turning his favourite pieces of music over in his mind. He knew just what he wanted.

Nurse Sims took his proffered piece of paper and glanced at it critically.

"What's this? The Scorpions? Never heard of 'em. What names you youngsters call yourselves! 'Winds of Change', is it?"

"It was high in the charts when I last heard it," Derek told her.

"Our Rosaleen'll know it, then." Nurse Sims bustled out. "We're all glad to have her back again, Mr Forder," she said over her shoulder. "Do you good, she will."

Precisely at ten-thirty, next day, just as Joe had said, the hospital radio came on. Derek, pushing his coffee cup aside, lay back, waiting.

"Hello, everybody!" The voice was warm and husky.

"Here I am back again, and yes, I had a super holiday. Now I'm here to play all your favourite numbers."

Derek listened intently. What a marvellous voice!

"Now let me see." He heard a rustle of papers. "There's a few names here I don't recognise.

"Derek Forder, you're new to this town, Nurse Sims tells me, and all alone in a side-ward. I'll start with your choice, then. The Scorpions. 'Winds of Change'."

Derek lay back, blissfully content and he began to picture the face that went with that warm, husky voice . . .

Dark hair, softly curling. Dark eyes to match. Rosaleen. He listened, entranced. Would she speak to him again?

She did.

"Enjoy that, did you, Derek? Hurry up and get better!"

"Well, laddie," Joe said on his next bedside visit. "Told you our Rosaleen was good, didn't I?"

Derek was lost for words.

"And fancy her singling you out!" Joe went on. "Some chaps have all the luck."

Derek wasn't slow in sending in his next request. And sure enough, it was played. Not singled out, of course. He couldn't hope for that again, but he listened eagerly for what Rosaleen would say.

"Another for our Derek in the side-ward. Hope you enjoy your music, Derek."

It wasn't just the record he enjoyed, it was the voice, too. Nobody had ever spoken to him in quite that warm, husky, special way.

On the third day, he added a postscript to his request.

Dear Rosaleen, he wrote, greatly daring. *Thanks a million.*

He folded the paper carefully lest Nurse Sims' eagle eye should see it, and waited for next morning.

TEN-THIRTY came, and Derek listened.

He was convinced she'd never reply. Yet when his request came on, there was the warm voice again:

"Thanks, Derek Forder in the side-ward. Nice to know you like the programme."

It was Sunday again before he dared to try another message.

Dear Rosaleen, he wrote. *I'm feeling better already, thanks to you. You can't guess what a difference you make to my day.* And signed it, *Love, Derek.*

Historic Scotland
THE MEMORIAL CAIRN, Culloden

THE Battle of Culloden was the last battle fought on the soil of the United Kingdom. In it, Bonnie Prince Charlie's army of Highlanders was defeated by a Hanoverian army led by the Duke of Cumberland. This was on April 16, 1746, and it ended the second Jacobite Rising.

The Memorial Cairn was built in 1881, and headstones were erected to identify the graves of the various clans which took part.

The Battlefield has been in the care of the National Trust for Scotland for the past 50 years, and there is a New Visitor Centre near the old, thatched Leanach Cottage.

No blame was ever cast on the Bonnie Prince. In his Highland wanderings in the aftermath of Culloden, men and women risked their lives to offer him succour and shelter, and many a fugitive with Cumberland's men at his heels was given sanctuary.

Their loyalty shone like a torch through the darkness that descended on Scotland after this great Jacobite defeat, in which a thousand Highlanders lost their lives. Although the whole fabric of the Highlands was shattered, the glamour inspired by Bonnie Prince Charlie remained, and the Jacobite songs and the romance of the tartans have never faded.

F

She won't mention it, he told himself, but fell asleep hoping she would.

The next morning, there was that warm voice again. He had to wait for his name this time.

"Glad you're on the mend, Derek. Hurry up and get better, for my sake!"

For my sake! Derek repeated the words, over and over again. Rosaleen was much more than a voice now. She was a person. The girl with the lovely voice . . .

But what did she look like? He found himself thinking, wondering, again and again. If only they could meet.

It was Joe who put paid to that. Ambling in without his crutches, he looked across approvingly at Derek, up and about in his bedside chair.

Joe seated himself uncomfortably on the bed, and grinned.

"Glad to see you up, laddie. I've come to say goodbye. Off tomorrow, I am. And am I glad! It'll be great to be home again with the wife and kids."

Derek felt a moment's envy. Someone with a family. Then he pulled himself together.

"That's good news, Joe. I'll miss you."

"I'll miss you, too," Joe said. "And Rosaleen. I'll miss that wonderful voice of hers."

"Does she ever meet her patients?" Derek asked hopefully.

"Never has, ever," Joe told him. "Plenty of us'd like to see her, but she never comes round the wards."

He rose.

"Well, so long, laddie. See you in the morning before I go."

A voice on the radio, Derek thought, sitting there disconsolately after Joe had gone. A voice, nothing more. And never would be.

YOU'LL be going out soon, Mr Forder," Nurse Sims told him the following Monday. "Doctor tells me you've been doing so well."

She eyed him closely. "Not a bit like you were when you first came in."

That's Rosaleen, Derek told himself. That's what she'd done for me.

"Now don't you go smashing yourself up again, young man," Nurse Sims added briskly. "You mightn't be so lucky next time. Got anyone to look after you at home?"

"My landlady," Derek said.

"Hm." Nurse Sims raised an eyebrow. "We'll get you a taxi for twelve o'clock on Wednesday morning."

Wednesday, Derek thought when she had gone. How could he leave the hospital without saying goodbye to Rosaleen?

On Tuesday morning his request was played as usual. For the last time, he told himself. Or — was it the last time?

He wasn't due to leave till twelve the next day. Still time to listen to the programme. He thought hard and long. It was now or never. *Dear Rosaleen*, he wrote on his note, his hand shaking a little. *Will you do something for me, please? Play your own choice tomorrow. I'd like to know which is your favourite number.*

And something else. I'll be going out at twelve tomorrow — just after your programme. You wouldn't, would you, meet me before I go? I'll be in the lobby.

Please.

And ended it: *Love, Derek.*

He spent a sleepless night. Of course, she wouldn't be there. Joe had told him that. And yet — he could always hope.

By ten-thirty he was sitting in the bedside chair, his case packed beside him. Nurse Sims glanced at him coolly.

"You haven't drunk your coffee, Mr Forder. I know you're going out soon, but there's no need to waste good coffee."

Derek drank it without thinking. Any moment now the radio would come on, and he wanted Nurse Sims out of the way. He waited, tense.

"Hello, everybody!"

His heart thumped. Had Rosaleen got his message? Would there be a special word for him, on this, his last day?

There was. Right at the end when he'd given up hope.

"And now it's goodbye to someone in that side-ward who's off home today. I still remember your first request, Derek. 'Winds of Change', wasn't it?"

Did he imagine a special warmth in that familiar voice?

"Well, now, you've left the choice to me, and here it is. 'Anything I do, I do for you'."

Anything I do! Derek listened, only half-believing. She understood! Did that mean she was going to meet him? The programme ended, and he glanced at his watch. Just after eleven-thirty. In less than half an hour he'd be leaving. She must come. She must!

Five minutes later he was sitting in the lobby, suitcase in hand.

He looked around. Plenty of people were crossing and re-crossing the polished floor. Which one of them was Rosaleen?

He could see no-one who looked like her at all. He waited, watching the clock.

Eleven forty. Eleven forty-five. She wasn't coming. Eleven fifty.

Only a couple of patients standing ready to leave; a doctor hurrying by; two nurses in uniform. No Rosaleen.

THEN a small figure detached itself from the others and walked towards him, holding out her hand.

Derek stared. This dumpy little person, round and smiling, with greying hair, was old enough to be his mother! In fact, she did look like his mother, as he could just remember her. Comfortable, kindly. His head began to whirl.

He felt his hand clasped with an unexpected warmth.

"You must be Derek. Derek from the side-ward. Glad to meet

you, Derek."

He swallowed hard. "Sorry, I — I — "

She finished for him. "Didn't think I'd look like this?" Her eyes twinkled.

Derek suddenly found himself returning that lovely smile.

"You've got such a marvellous voice, er — Rosaleen," he managed.

"Rosie, please. That's what they call me at home. Suits me better, don't you think?

"I'm so glad you liked my programme. I don't usually meet any of my patients, but I must confess I've had a very soft spot for you, Derek. Maybe because you're all alone."

Derek took both her hands in his.

"You've been wonderful to me, Rosie. I'd never have got better so soon if it hadn't been for you."

She smiled again. "I'm glad we met. Oh, just a moment — I think that's for me."

There was a little stir in the lobby as someone rushed through the doors. Looking over her shoulder, Derek saw a girl. A girl in a red coat, with dark, flying hair.

"Sorry I'm late, Mum," she panted. "Traffic was awful. I thought I'd missed you."

She stopped abruptly, seeing Derek. "Sorry — am I interrupting?"

Rosaleen stepped forward.

"Not at all. Jane, this is Mr Forder, who's leaving today. Derek and I were just saying goodbye. Derek, my daughter. She gives me a lift home."

Derek gasped and gazed at the girl. The same warm, husky voice. The dark hair and dark eyes of his dreams.

"Derek's been listening to my programme for weeks," Rosaleen went on. "I think — I hope — I've helped him to get better. It's no fun having nobody to visit you — is it?"

The girl turned on him her own warm smile, so like her mother's. "Where do you live, Mr Forder?"

Derek came out of his dreams.

"Er — I'm in digs. Nelson Street." He glanced towards the doors. "There'll be a taxi waiting for me . . ."

"Don't bother," Jane said. "I'm sure someone else will take it."

She took his arm with one hand, his case with the other. "I know Nelson Street. It's not far out of our way. No bother."

"Oh, but I couldn't!" Derek heard himself say.

Then her eyes met his. Was it possible she felt the same way he did? As if something new and wonderful was just beginning?

"It's kind of you," he said, looking from one to the other. A lovely lady. Two lovely ladies.

Then he turned to Jane. "If you really mean it — "

"Oh, but I do!" she said.

And from the warmth in that husky voice, Derek suddenly felt certain that she did. □

From The Heart

by CERI EVANS

GILL was a bit puzzled as she watched her daughter at breakfast. It was the first time since Sara had started her Saturday job that she'd been out of bed without a protest. And smiling, too! More to herself than to Gill, a private smile, as if she had a happy little secret safely tucked away.

It was a shame, Gill thought, that Sara had to give up her precious free time like this. At fourteen, life should really be care-free.

But there were only the two of them, and money was tight. Gill blamed herself for this development. It had been her idea to give up a steady job and come back to her home town. She'd lived so long with that deep yearning to go back and finally she'd given in.

Their life could have been so different if only she hadn't married Tim. If only . . . but no, she scolded herself, brushing her thoughts aside.

She'd hoped to get a good job here, but all she'd found was part-time work, enough to pay the bills though there was barely anything left over for luxuries. Poor Sara had to pay her own way when it came to all those little fripperies of teenage fun.

Not that she ever complained, for she enjoyed her work. The pet shop fascinated her and she adored the animals. The only thing that spoiled it was the man she worked for. Old Mr Hemmings was the meanest and grumpiest man imaginable. The only thing he seemed to be interested in was how much money was put into the till. He didn't care about the animals and that upset Sara.

It was surprising, then, to see her almost dancing off to town this morning. Perhaps, Gill thought, grouchy Mr Hemmings had re-formed. It was a nice idea but she didn't believe it one little bit! Sara was in love, more likely. Gill sighed. The time was bound to come . . . She crossed her fingers and prayed silently her daughter wouldn't find her first encounter painful . . .

★   ★   ★   ★

The only person on Sara's mind, however, was her mum. Tomorrow was her birthday and it was to be a special one. For so long now her mum had been unable to spend much money on herself. Sara was determined that this birthday would be different. She'd been saving ever since she started work for Mr Hemmings. He didn't pay her much and it had been a long struggle, but at least she'd reached her goal.

It was a good nine months since she'd seen the earrings in the jeweller's window. The moment they caught her eye, she knew they would make a perfect birthday present.

She'd emptied out her china pig and offered three months' wages as a deposit, with the promise of a few pounds more every week. The jeweller had smiled and taken the earrings out of the window and stored them in the back shop. She'd paid the last instalment two weeks ago, but for safety's sake she'd left them with him. And now, today, she was collecting them!

The feeling of excitement was unbearable — she couldn't possibly wait till evening. Instead, she'd risk a row for being late and pick up the earrings before she made her way to the pet shop. It would be great to have the tiny box with her all day and know that it was really hers.

At lunchtime she would choose a card — if she got a break. Old Mr Hemmings might want her to work her lunch break to make up for being late. Not that it mattered too much, the stationer's were always open late.

From The Heart

L UCKILY, Mr Hemmings wasn't there when she arrived. Molly, the kindly, middle-aged assistant, was standing in the doorway idly flicking through a magazine.

"You're living dangerously." Molly grinned. "I've never known him not be in on time before."

"I've been to get my mother's birthday present," Sara panted, still breathless from having to run. "Earrings."

"Ooh! Come on, let's have a look."

But Molly didn't get the chance. She'd spotted Mr Hemmings coming towards them.

"Never seen the town this bad for traffic before," their employer muttered moodily as he unlocked the door. "Couldn't park within a half a mile of the shop. If it gets any worse I'd be just as well to walk the whole way."

That set the tone for the whole morning. Mr Hemmings sat brooding by the till and watching while Sara and Molly worked. Occasionally he stirred himself long enough to ring up purchases on the till.

It was nearly ten o'clock when Sara noticed something odd.

"What's this?" she murmured, bending down and peering into a wire basket that lay under the counter. "A cat? I thought he didn't keep fully grown animals in the shop."

"He isn't selling that one," Molly explained. "I've a fortnight to find a home for her, or else . . ."

"But where'd she come from?"

Molly shrugged.

"I've no idea. I simply found her on Monday morning when I opened up the shop. Somebody had left her on the doorstep."

"But why . . . ?"

"Why does anyone abandon animals? I don't know. But I think in her case I can guess."

Sara glanced up, bewildered.

"She's going to have kittens, love. Whoever owned her couldn't have been pleased by that. Still, she's safe here for a bit, so long as I'm prepared to pay for her food and milk. I'd have taken her home myself, but there's the dog."

Molly put her fingers through the bars and gently stroked the white cat.

"I'll take her," Sara offered eagerly. "I'm sure Mum wouldn't mind. She's just as soppy about animals as I am."

"You've only got a flat, love, and I don't think your landlord would be too pleased."

"He wouldn't know — I wouldn't tell him."

Molly smiled, but sadly, touched by the girl's naivete.

"You couldn't keep her hidden long, Sara, and what'll you do once the kittens arrive?"

"When will she have them?"

"Don't know for sure, but I'd have thought fairly soon. She's very plump."

"I wonder if she's got a name," said Sara idly, as she, too, poked her fingers through the bars to stroke the cat.

"I'd call her Snowy, like most white cats," said Molly ruefully, "except I've a nasty feeling that she isn't."

★　　　★　　　★　　　★

Whenever she had a spare minute, Sara couldn't help but stroke the cat, delighting in the purring that now welcomed her. Just before midday, though, she noticed a change.

"Molly!" she called, regardless of Mr Hemmings' grim expression. "There's something wrong."

Molly peered anxiously into the cage, then straightened up and smiled.

"There's nothing wrong. It's just the kittens are ready to be born."

Sara, motionless and silent, watched with wonderment as the first small bundle came into the world and squirmed as its mother nuzzled it. Sara waited and waited, but nothing more happened. An hour passed and still the other kittens hadn't been born.

"Molly, I think there's something wrong, nothing's happening and she's trying so hard."

The older woman watched a moment, then she nodded.

D.I.Y.

WHEN he's got a job
　　To tackle —
There are lots of
Jobs for me!
Tools to find
(Domestic kind)
And non-stop cups of tea.
If a job is worth
The doing —
It must not be
Done in haste
Quotes the mighty
Master-Mender
(Putting me into
My place).
So, I stand here
At the ready,
Full of hope and eagerness . . .
To commence the Grand Finale —
Which is clearing up the mess!

Gaye Wilson.

DAWN CHORUS

*S*HADOWS *of night are fading*
  Over the garden fair,
And a single call
Both clear and high,
Startles the still air.
And now an answering call
Comes back
And another voice is heard.
Then comes a mighty chorus
Led by a lone song-bird.
This symphony of sound imparts
A burst of joy in human hearts.

Gaye Wilson.

"I think you're right, Sara, it shouldn't be like that."

"We ought to get a vet," said Sara. "There's that one just two streets away. It wouldn't take a minute to go round and fetch him."

"I'm not paying for any vet," Mr Hemmings muttered, getting up and reaching for his coat. "Just leave the animals alone and keep an eye on the shop. That's what you're paid to do.

"But mind you keep them kittens. They'll be worth a few pounds each to me. I'm going for lunch."

"And we're going for the vet!" Sara exclaimed the moment he was out of sight.

"There won't be a surgery on Saturday."

"I hadn't thought of that." Then suddenly she brightened. "There's bound to be a notice outside giving a number in case of emergencies. I could ring that."

"It's worth a try. You go. But run! I'll comfort little mother here."

But Sara was already through the door and haring up the road.

IT'S lucky I'd come in to get some papers," Mr Harris said, when she'd finished telling him about the cat. "Just let me get my bag."

He sounded calm and competent and Sara breathed more easily.

He seemed less confident, however, when he reached the shop.
"I think I'd better take her to the surgery. She needs more help than I realised."
"I'd like to come, too."
Mr Harris smiled and shook his head.
"You'd better not, but you could drop in and see her when you finish work, if you like."
After work Sara dashed round to the vet. Five fluffy kittens lay beside their mother, their tiny noses buried in her fur.
"They're gorgeous," Sara breathed.
She stood entranced watching the little bundles feeding, then, as one by one their hunger was satisfied, falling fast asleep. And then she came back to reality.
"The bill . . ." she ventured.
"I've made it out. If you'll just fill in this bit here. Name and address."
She took his pen and printed it carefully.
"Sara Gillespie-Barnes," the vet said, gazing at her thoughtfully. "That's an unusual name."
She nodded. Then she swallowed hard.
"I haven't that much money," she began.
He smiled.
"Don't worry. I'll send it on. Just put down your father's christian name."
"I haven't got a father," Sara murmured.
"Your mother's then."
"She couldn't possibly afford . . ."
The words came tumbling out.
"I mean, I know she'd find the money somehow, but . . ." she stumbled. "If I could pay instead."
The tears were stinging at her eyes. How could she pay a sum like that? Then an idea struck her. Fishing in her jeans, she found the box and gave it to him.
"Ernest Devine, Jeweller," he read, astonished.
"Open it," she urged.
Two teardrop pearls glowed softly against the purple velvet lining.
"They're real and they cost a lot. I've saved a whole year's money to buy them, so they'd be worth more than I owe you.
"They're for my mother's birthday. It's tomorrow. But I thought if I could leave them with you as a promise and then pay the bill off bit by bit . . ."
She stopped, aware that he was staring at her. Although she did not realise it, his thoughts were of another time, another girl, a little older maybe, yet with that same shade of auburn hair with golden tints, those same clear blue eyes . . . Surely, surely there was no mistaking striking looks like that. He shook his head.
"But then there'd be no birthday present," he said slowly.
"Mum wouldn't mind. She'd understand."
"It's hardly fair. The cat belongs to no-one, so no-one should have

to pay the bill."

He winked at Sara as he threw the crumpled paper in the bin.

After she'd gone he bent and carefully retrieved it. He could be wrong, of course.

And yet that name, and the striking resemblance . . .

He turned the car and headed for the edge of town. The shops there stayed open late.

NEXT morning Gill was standing by the mirror admiring her earrings, thinking to herself how lucky and proud she was to have such a caring, thoughtful daughter, then the doorbell rang.

"It's Mr Harris," Sara said excitedly.

Then suddenly her face went pale.

"Oh, Mum! There must be something wrong. The cat! Those lovely kittens . . ."

But Mr Harris was all smiles. The cat, he told her, was a perfect mother and the kittens, well, they were the finest he'd ever seen. He'd take her to see for herself later, though first he'd like to meet her mother.

Sara beamed, for he was standing awkwardly with one hand behind his back and she had glimpsed one stray red rosebud peeping out. How lovely that he'd remembered what a special day it was.

"Geoff!" Gill exclaimed as Sara led him in. "Geoff Harris!"

"Happy birthday," he said gently, producing the bouquet.

"But how did you know that I was living here?"

"It was your daughter. Once glance at her . . . I didn't think there could be many families with hair that colour." He smiled. "And when she wrote her name — and I realised you were on your own . . ."

Gill reddened slightly.

"It didn't work. Tim left when Sara was only two months old. We've been on our own ever since, though we only returned here recently."

"You should have looked me up."

"I wanted to. I truly did. But, well, I somehow just assumed that you would have met someone else and settled down."

"I never did, Gill. Perhaps because I wasn't looking. I only ever wanted you. You and my work. And when you married Tim, that just left my work."

Sara, coming from the kitchen with a vase, got half-way across the hall and stopped.

It was, as she confided later to the cat, more than surprising to see Mr Harris and her mum sitting so closely together and talking in a way that somehow didn't include her.

"There's a surprise for you as well," she murmured, fondling the soft white fur.

"I think there'll be a family for you and your kittens to come to soon. We've been made for each other!" □

THE MAN

W HEN I was six years of age, I thought my Uncle George was witty, wise and wonderful. Yet, by the time I reached sixteen, he seemed to me the most boring person on earth.

Poor Uncle George — his only fault was that he was so predictable! He never said anything that hadn't been said before . . . and very many times at that.

Uncle George and Aunt Dorothy were regular visitors at our house, and were nice, easygoing people you didn't have to impress. There was never any of that, "Tidy away your toys,

and don't mess up the bathroom. And for goodness' sake behave yourself, because Auntie and Uncle are coming!" They fitted in too well for that.

Dad's only brother, and several years his senior, Uncle George was a rosy-faced, tubby little man, rather like a good-natured gnome. His blue eyes were gentle and child-like, and he was unfailingly kind.

Aunt Dorothy was delicate and a bit olde-worlde, with a long, pale face and smooth, brown hair parted in the middle. I often thought she could have stepped out of some old picture. She never said much, but just sat there knitting — we all received the most marvellous jumpers and cardigans and pullovers from her at Christmas and on our birthdays.

We were quite content to have Uncle George and Aunt Dorothy so near us. They were the only relatives we needed — though I felt differently later on.

As a small child I was very awkward, for ever falling over things, or off things, or bumping into things. It was often Uncle George, who always seemed to be there when he was needed, who'd pick me up and dust me down.

"There, there, Susanna," he'd murmur soothingly, when I

WHO WAS ALWAYS THERE

by
KATHLEEN
O'FARRELL

fell off the swing. "Accidents will happen, you know, to the best of people." And he'd put a plaster on my knee, or find a penny so that its coldness would bring out the bump on my forehead.

When I got my first bike with pumped-up tyres, it was good old Uncle George who mended the punctures until I'd learned how.

"Actions speak louder than words," he'd declare, whipping off the tyre to plunge it into a bowl of cold water, to find just where the patch was needed.

Sadly, although they'd have made the kindest of parents, Uncle George and Aunt Dorothy had no children of their own. They lived in a neat, detached house in Woodland Walk, at the better-off end of Larchborough.

How I loved that house! It had the prettiest garden ever, with tall, slender silver birches on either side of the house, while a crazy-paving path, bordered with pinks and lavender, led to the front door. In the back garden were vegetables of all kinds, with fruit bushes, and rhubarb, masses of rosy phlox and sweetpeas, my favourite flowers.

Uncle George won prizes with his sweetpeas at the local flower show.

He and Aunt Dorothy didn't go out very much. "East, West, home's best!" Uncle George often reminded us. They never missed the flower show, though.

Although their house was lovely, they didn't mind children

rampaging about in it and often invited us over. My sister, Julie, my brother, Paul, and myself never refused. It was a heavenly place to visit.

Nobody grumbled at us if we ate the raspberries or blackcurrants, or climbed the apple trees. We enjoyed being fussed over, with gorgeous cakes for tea, that Aunt Dorothy made specially for us.

Sometimes we'd even stay a few days, and sleep in a charming bedroom overlooking the back garden. The walls were willow green, with a frieze of daisies, and the sort of pictures children like.

"This was to have been the nursery," Aunt Dorothy confided to me once. "Only we've never been blessed with little ones."

UNCLE GEORGE was regarded as the philosopher of the family and was quite unlike my father. How could two brothers be so different? They'd always been opposite, it seemed, right from schooldays.

"Your dad was a real imp when he was young," Uncle George told me once. "Always one for high jinks."

I smiled to myself, wondering what would constitute high jinks in Uncle George's estimation. Dear, funny old Uncle George, there was something so innocent about him.

I think I was his favourite. He'd call me "Sweet Susanna," and say my hair was the colour of marigolds. He was always ready to offer consolation and encouragement when things had gone wrong, or I had a bad report from school.

Julie and Paul were good at school, but I wasn't — I think I took after Dad. *Susanna must work harder to realise her full potential*, or *Susanna doesn't seem able to concentrate for very long*, were my teachers' comments.

At the time, I saw him as my champion and loved him for it. As I grew older, and a bit wiser myself, his proverbs began to pall. Sometimes, when he trotted out his "pearls of wisdom" as Aunt Dorothy naïvely called them, I found them very irritating, especially when I'd heard them a hundred times before.

Mum was much more blunt and to the point.

"You'll have to pull your socks up, Susie," she warned me, when my 'O'-levels were coming up. "You won't do as well as Julie and Paul did, not unless you cut out some of these discos and knuckle down to your homework."

For a while I really did try, because, although I knew I'd never be Brain of Britain, I did want to be *something* when I left school. Maybe an air hostess, or a hotel receptionist, or an assistant in a smart boutique, with lovely clothes all around me.

Julie and Paul had both gone on to college, but I didn't aspire to that.

It was just as well that I didn't, for I'd never have got there . . .

My good resolutions didn't last very long. I succumbed to all the distractions there were for a teenager at that time, and my "O"-level results were very poor.

Historic Scotland

GLENFINNAN —
Rallying Point of the Clans

BEAUTIFUL, romantic! Few would disagree with these descriptive words in visiting this perfect West Highland scene at Glenfinnan, at the head of Loch Shiel.

Here, in a lovely setting of loch and mountain, stands the stone tower commemorating the rallying point of the clans on August 19, 1745, at the start of the second Jacobite rebellion. And it was from Glenfinnan that the march southwards began, led by Cameron of Lochiel and his clansmen, ready to fight for Bonnie Prince Charlie.

The tower was erected in 1815 by Macdonald of Glenaladale (grandson of one of the Prince's original supporters) as a tribute to the clansmen who fought so bravely in the Jacobite cause. They are symbolised by the statue of a Highland clansman surmounting the monument. On plaques around the encircling wall is a dedication in three languages — Gaelic, English and Latin.

The monument, so simple yet so effective, is now in the care of the National Trust for Scotland.

"Never mind, Susie," Dad said, when I was in tears because my two best friends had done so much better than me. "You can stay on, and take them again next year."

Mum told me plainly that it was sheer laziness on my part. I'd have done much better, she said, if I'd had a bit more self-discipline.

EVEN second-time round, my "O"-levels were nothing to boast of. I found it very hard to obtain the sort of job I wanted. There was so much competition, and I bitterly regretted my previous happy-go-lucky attitude.

Uncle George still came round, full of sympathy and encouragement and loving kindness — which I didn't want.

One day I found him particularly trying. I'd just had a letter informing me that I hadn't got a job I'd been specially keen on. I felt angry and hurt and so disappointed I could have cried . . .

"Cheer up, Susanna," Uncle George said. "Remember, if at first you don't succeed, try, try, and try again!"

This was too much. I just couldn't take it . . .

"Uncle George," I muttered, "can't you just keep quiet? You and your boring old platitudes! I'm sick of them!"

Then I ran out of the room and up the stairs, for a really good cry in the privacy of my bedroom.

Looking back on that scene, I am deeply ashamed. I'd never spoken to Uncle George like that before — and never did again.

The look on his rosy, innocent face haunted me. Pain, mixed with disbelief . . .

Next day he brought me round a great big beautiful bunch of sweetpeas, as a sort of peace offering. And he hadn't done anything wrong . . .

Of course, I found work eventually, compiling patients' records for our family doctor. It was interesting and satisfying work, and after a couple of years I became receptionist. For a while I was very happy.

Paul had joined the Navy, and quiet, sensible Julie had become a teacher and married a fellow teacher. I was the only one at home and I'd sobered down a lot by then — partly because of my job.

But I still had my moments — and in one of these I fell in love!

Sadly, there was a shadow over my wedding. Dad had been made redundant.

He was shattered. Mum and he were often to be found whispering together, and I had a feeling that something momentous was going to happen.

My fears were only too well-founded. John and I had been married and settled into our nice little semi-detached house for only a month or two, when Mum and Dad announced that they were emigrating to Australia.

It seemed they had finally succumbed to the persuasion which Mum's sister, our Aunt Jessie and her husband, Uncle Dan, had been exerting for years. Mum was very fond of her sister, and as there was a job for Dad in Uncle Dan's business, we couldn't really blame them for their decision.

But, oh, I did miss them! It didn't affect my brother and sister so much. Paul was in mid-ocean and very happy in his chosen career, while Julie and her husband had moved miles from Larchborough, and were busy setting to rights an old cottage with a huge garden.

Aunt Dorothy and Uncle George felt the separation keenly, too, though not one word did they say to stop Mum and Dad going. On the contrary . . .

"Nothing ventured, nothing gained," Uncle George proclaimed, blinking away the tears when they came to say goodbye.

He promised them, very solemnly, that he would keep an eye on "Sweet Susanna" for them. I thought it funny and rather touching that he should still feel protective towards me, even though I was happily married.

The time was to come, though, when I would be only too glad of Uncle George's kindly concern. Only five years later my cosy little world fell apart . . .

A T the age of twenty-four, I was suddenly widowed. My dear, gentle John was on his way home from work one murky autumn evening when he was knocked from his bicycle. When I got the news I was at home, putting our two babies to bed. Little Becky was two and a half, and Ben was only six months . . .

The Man Who Was Always There

The whole family was devastated by the news. Mum and Dad flew back for the funeral, and begged me to return to Australia with them. But I didn't want to leave Larchborough, where I'd been happy for so long.

Later on, though, I wondered if I should have gone.

Somehow, by being almost idiotically brave for the sake of the children, I managed to get through that first year without John. But the years that followed were bleak indeed. How hard it was — the loneliness, the poverty, the having to make-do all the time.

With Mum and Dad and Paul so far away and Julie with her own family, I had no-one to turn to. Except Uncle George.

He was wonderful. Ben and Becky went wild when he came through the door with flowers, fruit and vegetables from his garden and a couple of their favourite chocolate bars.

Aunt Dorothy was kind, too. She knitted beautiful woollies for the children, and made fantastic birthday cakes in the shape of fairy-tale houses or trains.

But, although Uncle George sometimes offered me financial help, I never accepted it. Even when I was worried sick about the final reminders stuck behind the clock . . . Even when we lost our home and had to move into a horrid, poky flat where the people below complained ceaselessly about the children . . . My pride, or pig-headedness, kept me going . . .

If only I could have taken a job! But the children were too young to leave, and Ben was often ill and needed extra mothering.

We lived on make-believe in those days . . . I didn't mind going without things myself, but I was determined my children should have a reasonably happy childhood to look back on. Fortunately, they were easily pleased and quite unspoilt.

What would we have done without Uncle George, though? Even while he irritated me with his worn-out old maxims, he was invaluable to us.

Sometimes, in dark moments, I thought longingly of Uncle George's lovely house, with only the two of them in it. And the big garden, the fruit bushes, and all those glorious flowers . . . Just suppose . . . Just suppose he offered us a room or two there one day . . . Would I accept? Or would the prospect of living under the same roof as Uncle George be too daunting?

I'd snapped his head off once and had often been tempted to again, yet he really didn't deserve it . . .

He was retired by then, and didn't look so dapper any more. Almost overnight, it seemed, the jolly, tubby, rosy-faced gnome had changed into a smaller, more elderly one, with wistful eyes. Besides fretting about Aunt Dorothy, who was becoming increasingly frail, I think he missed our dad a lot.

Aunt Dorothy still knitted all the time, and never complained or made a fuss. But now her gentle face had a different sort of pallor, like a white rose when it starts to go creamy-brown around the edges. No wonder Uncle George was concerned. They had always been so

The Farmer And His Wife

by John Taylor

ANNE and I have a soft spot for two places in the North of England.

One is the beautiful area bordering the banks of a famous salmon river, the Lune. It has the most picturesque bridge, in my eyes, in the North of England — the Devil's Bridge.

Anne says that at the back of my mind I have more useless information than any man she knows. Well, as I hope she doesn't know other men as well as John Taylor, they can't know much!

The other area we like, although as we grow older our visits are too far between, is around Ullswater.

I think I told you our family knew of our love for this area, and gifted us a four-day break at one of the hotels on the lake side, on the occasion of our golden wedding.

Whenever the family travel in that direction, they never fail to bring us old folk a present each. It's a difficult problem, as Anne and I know from past years when we tried to think what to give our respective parents.

The family's gifts to us are simple, but bought with care and thought.

Anne and I have been given useful presents — Cumberland sausages, brandy butter, small cheeses and books for me. They all know I am interested in food — and reading.

A NUMBER of years back, on their return, they handed me a book entitled, "A Taste of the Lake District." I thanked them and said I would read it later. That, I think, was five years or so ago.

One evening when Anne decided to have an evening of polishing copper and brass, she said, "John, will you bring that coal-scuttle out of the bathroom?"

Don't laugh — there's no coal in it. Over the years, Anne has collected brass and copper, and her last two purchases were copper coal-scuttles — for the boys when they got married.

close, those two. I don't believe they had ever quarrelled, in all their years together.

But then, Aunt Dorothy adored my uncle. To her, he would always be witty, wise and wonderful. Not a well-intentioned, generous, kindly old *bore* . . .

I hated myself when I had uncharitable thoughts about Uncle George, because I really did love him and so did my children. But how desperately I longed for something to show me my uncle in a different light! If only he'd come out with one original remark, one little "pearl of wisdom" that was his, and his alone!

"Poor little Susie, it never rains but it pours," he'd declare, coming in when the pipes froze or Ben was coughing or Mrs Pyke was complaining about Becky skipping and singing.

Or: "Any little jobs for me to do, my sweet Susanna? You know what they say, about Satan and idle hands!"

Then, one March day, I had a surprise.

UNCLE GEORGE arrived, with a big bunch of yellow forsythia and suggested we moved in with Aunt Dorothy and himself!

I stared at him, not knowing what to say.

"But it wouldn't be fair," I pointed out, when I had marshalled my thoughts. "You and Aunt Dorothy don't want noisy youngsters rampaging about. You two want peace and quiet . . ."

But there, it seemed, I was quite wrong.

"You don't understand, Susie, my dear," he said, slowly and

What worries me, will the boys or their wives want the antiques that Anne is busy storing up or them? I have my doubts.

Well, this coal-scuttle in the bathroom has no coal, but magazines and books. I lifted these out, then paused.

Ah, there was my "Taste of the Lake District" . . .

"John, are you all right?" Anne called.

"Coming, dear," I replied reluctantly.

ONE Sunday afternoon in July, after a particularly enjoyable lunch, I took my "Taste of the Lake District" into the lounge.

It was 128 pages long, but on one side of each page was an old photograph taken about 1890 or so, and on the other side was a short story, then a Lake District recipe. Some would say I wasted a Sunday afternoon just reading, but many of the stories and recipes brought back memories of our early upbringing.

One of the photos was of Beatrix Potter. I suppose you, like me, had one or more of her beautifully illustrated books of animal tales.

Well, I learned from this book that she used the income from the sale of her books to buy farms where she bred those famous sheep of the Lake District — the Herdwicks. She went on to be Chairman of the Herdwick Sheep Breeders' Association.

It isn't always an expensive present which gives most enjoyment, is it?

"A Taste of the Lake District" cost £3.95, and I know that Anne and I will get hours of pleasure, not only reading the text, but learning how to deal with venison and other cuts of meat — the Cumberland way — for Anne's dinner parties for our friends.

thoughtfully, as he sat there with a child on either knee, his arms tight around them.

"People say silence is golden, but it isn't really. Not all the time. It can be dark and cold and empty, and quite frightening.

"And as for peace — true peace — that's something deep down inside you. If it's there, exterior things don't matter. Children laughing, or singing, or larking around, or even squabbling — sounds like those don't have any effect on real, inner peace. Not when it's the genuine thing. It's just like raindrops running off a flower petal!"

Was this really Uncle George talking?

"To tell the truth, Susie," he went on, solemnly, "I haven't felt at peace for some time now . . . seeing you and little Becky and Ben in this dreadful place.

"I've been wanting to say something for ages, because it would cut both ways, you see. You'd be able to run the house and take the strain off my dear Dorothy — she'd be overjoyed if you'd come. And you'd live rent free, and the little ones could have that nice room we still call the Children's Room . . . But . . ." His voice tailed off.

"I've been afraid to suggest it." he said quietly at last. "I suppose it's not much of an offer, really . . . It mightn't appeal to a smart, pretty girl like you."

A smart, pretty girl! When I hadn't bought a new dress in years, and felt at least a hundred and fifty! For a moment I was too stunned to speak.

"Oh, well, never mind." Mistaking my silence, Uncle George turned his head away.

When next he spoke his voice was gruff. "It was just an idea . . . a silly idea, perhaps. But you know what they say — there's no fool like an old fool . . ."

He set Becky and Ben down, and stood up, as if he were going. "No, Uncle George, no!" I cried. "You mustn't say that!"

Suddenly, my arms were around him and I was crying unashamedly.

"It's just that you took my breath away — I didn't know what to say. It's the most wonderful offer ever! But all the advantages seem to be on my side."

As I thought of that delightful house, with its charming Children's Room, and the garden, all damask roses and lavender and sweetpeas in the summer . . . why, it was just too much!

"Oh, Uncle George," I murmured, "dear Uncle George, I'm so grateful!"

"You needn't be." Uncle George's eyes were twinkling. "After all, we're only offering you a job as unpaid housekeeper — though all found, it's true, including holidays. We'll all go off to the sea in the summer . . ."

Then, quickly reverting to his old form, he added, "I should have plucked up courage and asked you long ago, with Dorothy getting so frail. Still, better late than never!"

And when he went on to remind me that blood was thicker than water, it no longer irritated me. From then on, Uncle George could say exactly what he liked. He was capable of much deeper, much lovelier, more original thoughts as well.

THAT was a few months ago. We've settled in very comfortably now, the children and I, and the arrangement works well.

While I run the house, and take most of the responsibility off Aunt Dorothy's shoulders, Uncle George potters in the garden, and plays games with Ben and Becky — he's just put up a swing for them, under the trees. I'm sure he hasn't been so happy for years, and the same goes for Aunt Dorothy, who's making the prettiest-ever mint-green jumper for Becky's birthday. As for me, I've started to feel young again . . .

"If you want to go out in the evening, Susie, you won't have to worry about baby-sitters." Aunt Dorothy has become my friend and confidante.

But I don't know about going out yet. My love for John is still there, like a rose pressed in some old book, sweet and delicate and fragrant — and enduring! Meanwhile, I'm making raspberry jam . . .

Ben and Becky are helping me, their eyes shining, their faces smeared with crimson juice. What sheer bliss it was, gathering those raspberries, all warm from the sun and smelling so utterly delicious! Little did I dream, this time last year, that I'd ever be as happy as this again.

But there, as good old Uncle George would say, it's a long lane that has no turning . . . □

Historic Scotland

TREASURE TROVE —
Tobermory Bay

S OME years late, in 'eighty-eight
As I do well remember,
(It was, some say, the nineteenth of May
And some say in September,
And some say in September)

The Spanish train launched forth amain
With many a fine bravado,
Their (as they thought, but it proved not)
Invincible Armado,
Invincible Armado.

The Queen was then at Tilbury
What could we more desire-a?
And Sir Francis Drake, for her sweet sake,
Did set them all on fire-a,
Did set them all on fire-a.

THE old song does not add that the Spanish galleons were scattered and that one of them, named Florida, found its way up the west coast of Scotland. Battered by storms, what was left of her found refuge in Tobermory Bay, Island of Mull.

Then, it is said, a local man, held as hostage, holed the vessel and sent her to the bottom, where she still lies well buried in the seabed.

The historic site might be called a going concern. The Florida was the Armada's flagship and treasure-ship, and from time to time attempts have been made to retrieve that treasure.

Already various articles have been salvaged, the biggest prize so far being a cannon, which was later taken to Inveraray Castle, but the treasure itself has still to be found.

No doubt further attempts will be made — sunken treasure has a fascination of its own.

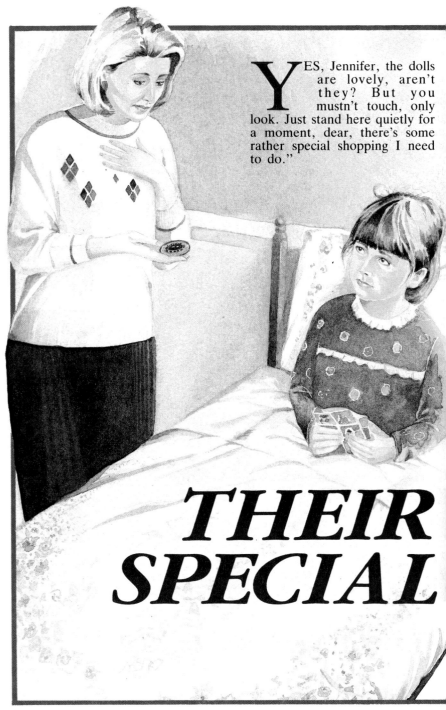

YES, Jennifer, the dolls are lovely, aren't they? But you mustn't touch, only look. Just stand here quietly for a moment, dear, there's some rather special shopping I need to do."

THEIR
SPECIAL

Clare waited for the inevitable question. Jennifer did not disappoint her.

"What are you going to buy?" she asked in her small, clear voice, which trembled with excitement.

Clare sighed as she glanced from her lengthy shopping-list to the eager face of the little girl beside her. It was hot and crowded in the toy department on that morning of Christmas Eve — and Clare felt harassed to say the least. Caring for children could be very exhausting!

But exhaustion was not her major problem. Just how, she wondered, did you buy an inquisitive five-year-old the stocking fillers which Father Christmas was supposed to bring, when the five-year-old in question was standing right beside you, watching your every move?

Just then, Clare caught sight of an ice-cream bar just a few yards away.

"Look, Jennifer," she coaxed, "suppose you buy yourself a lollipop — the kind with the creamy filling? Then you can suck it while you wait for me."

Clare rummaged in her bag and brought out a 50p piece which Jennifer accepted gratefully.

VERY
VISITOR

by ELIZABETH FARRANT

"But remember," Clare told her, "you must stay by the counter until I come to fetch you."

Jennifer trotted off contentedly to join the end of the little queue of children around the brightly-decorated ice-cream bar — and Clare gave a sigh of relief. It would give her the chance she needed, she told herself — though she wouldn't have much time.

She spotted a "Stocking Fillers" notice and proceeded to make her choice in record time. A drawing-pad and a box of coloured pencils . . . a family of yellow plastic ducks to sail in the bath . . . a Father Christmas filled with chocolate drops . . . a tiny frog which jumped each time you pressed it . . . a "magic" painting-book . . . a spinning-top . . .

It occurred to Clare that this was the very first time she'd been called upon to fill a Christmas stocking. She thought of the Christmas stockings of her own childhood . . . hanging forlornly in the glow of the lamplight before she fell asleep on Christmas Eve — yet bulging with exciting parcels when she opened her eyes early on Christmas morning. Strange how the memories came crowding back . . .

Forgetting her aching feet, she smiled to herself. Who would have thought, only a week ago, that she would be spending Christmas Eve morning shopping for *toys* of all things?

Only last night, she'd turned the idea down flat when her friend, Jean Farley, had appeared on her doorstep without a word of warning, suggesting a plan which at first had left Clare speechless.

"I'm very sorry, Jean," she'd answered firmly, when she'd had time to collect her thoughts a little. "But I'm afraid I just can't help . . . tomorrow's Christmas Eve, after all," she'd added. "I mean . . . it's such short notice.

"And besides," she'd concluded, "Charles and I — let's face it — we're just not used to having children around."

Jean ran her fingers through her short, dark hair which could have looked really good, Clare had often thought, if only she'd spare the time to have it properly styled. But Jean had no time to worry about her appearance. Children absorbed her constantly these days . . .

So different from Clare herself. Smart clothes and careful grooming, with attention to every important little detail, had long since become a way of life to her. She liked to look good — and, anyway, she owed it to Charles. He was doing well in his job with a local engineering firm and was now in line for a very good promotion. By the time he was thirty-five he could well be taking his place on the Board of Directors.

WHAT must it feel like to be Jean, she'd wondered. The two of them had been friends since their early schooldays — and Jean, as Clare would be the first to admit, was one of the kindest people she'd ever known.

Almost *too* kind, sometimes. As if three boisterous young children of her own weren't more than enough for even Jean to cope with, she'd had to volunteer to take another child into her home for Christmas. A five-year-old from the local children's home.

"And it's such bad luck," she'd sighed, "that two of my own should have gone down with chicken-pox — now of all times. Poor little Jennifer — she's been counting the days, the housemother says, till Christmas Eve. It'd mean so much to her to have a family Christmas."

And that, of course, was when Jean had first suggested that Jennifer might come to Clare instead.

But this, Clare told herself, just wasn't on. They'd made all their Christmas arrangements, she and Charles — planned everything well in advance, as they always did. They had no family ties, so on Christmas Day itself, they were eating out. It was quite the most sensible way of doing things, saving on all those lengthy preparations — to say nothing of all that tiresome clearing-up. No, no, they couldn't possibly take the child.

Clare's conscience had pricked her a little, all the same — and she suspected that it must have shown, though Jean had not given the smallest hint of reproof. She'd patted Clare's arm and given her a reassuring smile.

"Look, not to worry, love. I do understand, of course — it was just a thought," she'd said comfortingly, then glanced at her watch.

"Oh, no — is that the time? I've left Dave coping with the invalids — he's a great dad, but they'll be giving him a terrible time! They get so miserable when they're under the weather. You know what children are."

And Clare had smiled — a rueful little smile. That was just it, she'd thought — she *didn't* know . . .

But today she was learning fast.

It had been quite a trivial incident that had made her change her mind at the last moment. It was after she'd seen Jean off that it happened.

She'd stood for a moment in the open doorway, watching Jean go, her footsteps echoing along the frosty pavement.

It was two years since she and Charles had bought this large, old-fashioned cottage, a mile or so out of town, and employed a reliable firm to make all the necessary improvements. The house was looking at its very best tonight, Clare told herself, as she gazed at the dancing flames in the inglenook fireplace.

But that night she'd felt strangely restless. It was hard to remember that there'd been a time when she and Charles had longed for children, when they'd found themselves making plans for a family — even thinking of names.

It had been a great disappointment to them both when tests had proved that Clare could never have a baby of her own.

For a time, they'd considered adoption — but the waiting lists of would-be-adoptive parents were so long — the number of babies available so few. And somehow, as time went on, the thought had gradually ebbed from their minds.

P 108 ▶

LOCH LOMOND IN SNOW : J CAMPBELL KERR

YET the feeling of restlessness had persisted somehow, that night before Christmas Eve.

Unable to settle, Clare switched on the television in time to catch the end of an item in the local news — a Nativity play filmed in an infant school. Half absentmindedly at first, she'd found herself watching the usual Christmas pageant — the angels with tinselled wings, the shepherds, the Three Wise Men, Mary herself, a miniature Madonna, nursing the doll that represented the Baby Jesus . . .

"Christmas — a time of giving," the newscaster summed up. "And a special time for children everywhere."

But not for Jennifer — a persistent little voice had seemed to whisper.

Clare had switched off the television abruptly, an uneasy question forming in her mind. *What did she and Charles know about giving?*

It was then that on a sudden crazy impulse, she'd found herself lifting the receiver and dialling Jean's number.

"You *will* ?" Jean had gasped into the phone a moment later. "Thanks, Clare — you're an angel — I don't know how to thank you . . ." She'd paused for a moment. "You're sure it'll be all right? What about Charles?"

Good question, Clare had thought. Because, of course, she hadn't told him yet. She'd simply need to keep her fingers crossed and hope he'd understand.

He came home late and tired, after a busy day, but Clare could tell he was pretty pleased about something, all the same. And he gave her his news before she'd even had time to tell him hers.

"It's a bit of luck we're free on Christmas Eve," he'd told her jubilantly as he kissed her. "We'll need to be really on our toes. Just guess who's coming in for drinks? The Madisons, no less!"

"Why, love — that's wonderful, isn't it?" Clare had murmured.

Giles Madison was the senior partner of Charles's firm, a man of considerable influence. And Margot, his wife, had become a kind of

LOCH LOMOND IN SNOW

L OCH LOMOND is more usually photographed in sunshine, but as many devotees of this part of Scotland will know, it has its own charm on a crisp winter's day. Within easy reach of Glasgow, Loch Lomond and the surrounding countryside provide a mecca for lovers of the outdoors, whether they enjoy the spectacular scenery from the comfort of a car, or don walking gear to do battle with the elements.

◀ *over*

legend in the office. Smart, elegant, and almost alarmingly sophisticated, she was known for her way of summing up people at a first
glance, and for her shrewd grey eyes which noticed every detail . . .

"Christmas Eve?" Clare repeated faintly.

"That's right. They're spending Christmas with some friends down
south so, as they'll be driving past here just around seven, they
thought they might look in to say, 'Happy Christmas'!

"It was old Madison's idea, of course." Charles chuckled. "He was
in a pretty mellow mood today. Told me he'd heard about my lovely
wife and, you know, Clare, I just can't wait to show you off to them
both." He broke off suddenly as he saw the expression on her face.

"What's wrong, love? There's no need for you to panic. You'll
cope marvellously, you always do."

"I'm not panicking," Clare answered slowly. "Only — something's
cropped up. Something I hadn't bargained for, I mean."

And then she'd told him about Jennifer.

He'd stared at her for a moment, lost for words, then made for the
cocktail cabinet and poured himself a drink. "Good grief. You mean
she's coming *here? To stay?*"

"Only from Christmas Eve till Boxing Day," Clare faltered. "I felt
I couldn't refuse — it seemed so mean . . ."

"But what are we going to *do* with her all day?"

This was what Clare had begun to wonder, too — but she didn't
say so.

"Well, at least we'll have our evenings to ourselves," she coaxed
him. "And it needn't spoil *all* our plans. I mean — she'll be tucked
up in bed on Christmas Eve a long time before the Madisons arrive
. . . I'm sure it'll all work out."

BUT today, in the crowded store, clutching her parcels as she
paid her bill, Clare was feeling a lot less optimistic. It had been
a muddled, hectic kind of morning.

She and Charles had collected Jennifer from the children's home
quite early, and stopped for a little while to chat to the housemother,
a friendly, sympathetic woman Clare knew well — mainly through
Jean's activities, of course.

Then Charles had had to look in at the office, which had meant
Clare had to cope with Jennifer alone — and with all the extra
shopping.

Clare couldn't help thinking of all the jobs she'd left undone at
home. She'd meant to polish up her nicest glassware and to work on
some really special flower arrangements. She wished she could spare
the time to have her hair done. She'd need to look her very best
tonight . . .

She sighed to herself. There'd be no chance — she'd have to
entertain Jennifer this afternoon.

She glanced round sharply. Where *was* Jennifer? There was no sign
of her at the ice-cream bar.

Panic-stricken, Clare rushed to the entrance. The shop was immediately opposite an open market place and it was crammed with last-minute shoppers. Her heart thumped wildly as her eyes frantically scanned the crowds.

And then she saw her. A stolid little figure in her blue coat, threading her way among the market stalls.

The relief that swept over Clare almost made her feel faint. "Jennifer!" she gasped. "Where have you been?"

Jennifer didn't answer. Under her thick, dark fringe, her bright eyes gazed up unblinkingly. There was no sign of the lollipop, Clare noticed, but of course she'd have disposed of that long ago.

Clare didn't want to scold — she was too relieved to see the child. Her one desire was to get safely home.

Charles was already home when they arrived. Clare saw, to her surprise, that he looked quite cheerful as he greeted them, so she made no mention of the shopping incident.

"I picked up a Christmas tree and a box of decorations — oh, and some fairy lights, of course," he said. "And a few balloons . . . we always had balloons when we were kids at home — at Christmas, I mean," he added — rather sheepishly, Clare thought.

Jennifer ran indoors, her solemn little face alight with pleasure. And as Clare hurried off into the kitchen to prepare a hasty lunch, she heard her calling out ecstatically, "Let's blow the balloons up *now* !"

A moment later she heard Charles chuckling as Jennifer puffed at her balloon in vain, and the little girl's peals of laughter as Charles blew too hard and a balloon went "pop." It was a long time, Clare was thinking, since there'd been such raucous laughter in their home . . .

The decorating of the Christmas tree kept them absorbed for much of the afternoon, and when it was dark enough to switch on the fairy lights and they all stood back to admire the transformation, Clare

P 112 ▶

RYE, SUSSEX

*W*ITH *its narrow, cobbled streets and half-timbered houses, the East Sussex town of Rye gives the impression of being in an attractive "time warp." Rye has been associated with the Cinque Ports since the 12th century. A grassy terrace which has had cannon placed on it since Elizabethan times now has three cannon specially made to commemorate the 80th birthday of Queen Elizabeth the Queen Mother, Lord Warden of the Cinque Ports.*

RYE, SUSSEX : J CAMPBELL KERR

sensed a touch of magic in the air — a *Christmas* magic she hadn't felt for years. It was almost — almost as if they were a family.

But a glance at the clock brought her back sharply to reality. There was so much to do. The carpet was strewn with biscuit crumbs and littered with burst balloons and scraps of tinsel — and there were finger-marks on the polished furniture. By the time she'd made the room presentable, bathed Jennifer and got her into bed, there'd be scarcely time for her to have a quick shower and get herself ready for the Madisons.

"You must be fast asleep before Father Christmas comes," Clare told the little girl when at last she was tucked up in the spare room bed.

Jennifer's eyes, which were still wide open, had a thoughtful look.

"Does Father Christmas come to grown-up people?" she asked at last.

"Oh, no," Clare told her. "Only to girls and boys."

"That's what I thought." Jennifer nodded solemnly. "That's why I bought you this — I got it for you this morning in the market. It's a surprise . . ." she whispered.

Rummaging under her pillow, she pulled out a little crumpled paper bag and held it close to Clare.

Clare opened it, aware of those bright, dark eyes watching her anxiously.

Inside was a brooch — a very large one. A cluster of bright red beads in a pale pink plastic setting. Not only the largest brooch, but quite the most hideous Clare had ever seen.

"It cost me all my lollipop money," Jennifer told her proudly.

"Why, thank you, love — it's . . . beautiful," Clare murmured, a lump in her throat.

Jennifer's face lit up. "But you mustn't put it on," she insisted — "not yet. Not till you've changed into your party dress. *Then* you must show me."

Clare's heart sank at the very idea of pushing that clumsy pin through the delicate fabric of her new green dress. But she glanced at Jennifer's eager little face. To hurt the child's feelings would be worse — much worse, she thought. And of course, when she'd settled Jennifer down to sleep, she could remove the brooch and quickly substitute her favourite pendant . . .

But after the effect of the brooch on the dress had been duly approved and admired by Jennifer, there was the ceremony of hanging up her stocking — and by the time the final goodnights were said the door-bell was ringing — and Charles was letting the Madisons in.

FLUSTERED, Clare ran downstairs and found them already in the sitting-room — Giles tall and handsome and distinguished-looking, and Margot all unruffled elegance. And there was something in the atmosphere which told Clare at once that there was something wrong.

Charles, who was pouring the drinks, glanced up at her with a mixture of bewilderment and concern. Clare did her best to play the gracious hostess, but the feeling of strain was unmistakable. The Madisons kept up a polite, yet stilted conversation, but from time to time Clare was aware that Margot was giving her the oddest looks.

What could be wrong, Clare wondered miserably. One thing was certain, anyway, she thought — somehow she'd let Charles down. The visit had proved a failure, after all.

It was not till the Madisons were about to leave that she heard soft footsteps padding down the stairs — and the next moment Jennifer's face was peering round the door. Half-shyly, half-proudly, she made her way to Clare.

"I want to see the brooch again," she told her. "It's a good thing I picked the pink one, isn't it? It's *lovely* on your dress."

It was then, and only then that Clare remembered. The brooch — she'd forgotten to take it off!

Then everyone began to talk at once — it was almost like the breaking of a spell. All feelings of strain and embarrassment melted away.

"So the brooch was your Christmas present to your mummy?" Giles asked, with a sudden twinkle in his eye. "What a clever young lady to choose it by yourself!"

Margot turned to Clare with a sudden softness in her eyes as she murmured, "We never knew you had a little girl . . . treasure that brooch, my dear," she added quietly. "It was a gift of love."

"But . . . we haven't . . . she isn't . . ." Clare faltered uncertainly. Then she broke off, conscious that Jennifer was listening intently. No, this was not the time for explanations.

It was then that Clare found herself remembering something that the housemother at the home had said that morning.

"We're hoping that very soon we'll find a couple who'll give this child a long-term foster-home . . ."

After the Madisons had driven off and Jennifer was back in bed once more, Clare and Charles went upstairs together, to check that she'd settled down.

She was almost asleep, but she murmured drowsily, "I'm glad you liked the present." And she held out her arms for a hug.

Clare held her tightly.

"Know something, Jennifer?" she said. "It's just what I've always wanted." But now she wasn't thinking of the brooch.

She glanced at Charles and sensed that, like herself, he was thinking of another kind of gift. She reached for his hand and they sat by Jennifer's bedside very quietly till at last she fell asleep.

From somewhere in the distance Clare heard a Christmas carol and she glowed with a strange new feeling of contentment. Christmas was, after all, a time of giving. And the best time of all, she thought, for a gift of love. □

A World Of Difference

THE decorator smoothed the emulsion over the ceiling with strong, rhythmical strokes.

My nephew and I watched, mesmerised; Simon with the painting, me with the painter.

"My turn now!" the three-year-old insisted.

Alan Boon took his deep-brown eyes away from his work for a moment.

"Not the ceiling, Simon. It's too high. But you can help me with the walls tomorrow. If Auntie Laura agrees."

As I nodded my consent, Alan smiled at me, conspiratorially.

"I could play with him all day, you know."

That was quite obvious. I only wished that he felt the same way about me. But all Alan's attention was devoted to Simon who was playing with his smaller paint brushes, and tidying his work box.

All this had left me nearly redundant. I was supposed to be entertaining my nephew while my sister, Sarah, did some part-time work.

To be honest I'd been dreading the decorator coming to do her living-room. There would be such a mess and the weather was too cold to take Simon out for long. I needn't have worried, though, Simon rejoiced in the disorder. He raced his bike round the piled-up furniture in the middle of the living-room, and threw himself into helping with a will.

Simon would certainly miss Alan when he finished, which would be another three days at his present rate of progress. So would I.

by HELENA CHAMBERS

Even from the first moment I saw Alan, half-way up his ladder, his dark hair prematurely whitened with flecks of paint, I felt a surge of curiosity and attraction. His tall figure had the effortless strength of a man whose work is physical, but his hands were delicate and fine. And at first, I had been optimistic that he might feel the same about me.

Getting to know him had been so easy, so natural. We chatted comfortably about odd things: a song on the radio, the spring beauty of the trees in the garden.

When he arrived in the morning I used to make him a cup of tea — strong but milky — and somehow quite a domestic atmosphere developed between us. But then he seemed to draw back from it.

"What do you intend to do with your life?" he had asked me, at the end of the first week. "Work with children?"

"No, I'm at college learning to be a personal assistant."

"Who are you going to assist? A managing director?" he queried.

"That's the idea."

"Good for you. Aim for the top!" He smiled ruefully. "Everything's possible at your age."

A S the days passed I noticed that he often mentioned the difference in our ages. I became too annoyed not to retaliate. "You talk like my grandfather!" I accused him. "How old are you, anyway?"

"Twenty-nine," he admitted. "Over ten years older than you."

"Not quite," I corrected him. "And women mature earlier than men."

He smiled.

"Perhaps. But ten years of working, making your own way in the world, make a lot of difference."

I felt slighted. I wished I hadn't told him that I was still living with my parents. Now he just thought of me as a child.

"What's your career ambition?" I challenged him.

"My own interior design and decorating service. Advice on colour schemes, materials, design and co-ordination of furniture, everything.

"I aim to do the whole job, right from the planning stage. It's been difficult — starting out — but I'm gradually getting the sort of business I want."

The determination in his tone assured me he would succeed.

"Don't go broadcasting my master-plan," he warned. "There's such a thing as industrial espionage, you know."

It was typical of him to joke about it, but I got the impression he did not talk about his cherished plans lightly. That was why it was so hard to tell what he thought of me. One moment he would dismiss me as barely out of kindergarten, and the next he'd treat me as a confidante.

As the days progressed, his manner became more distant and formal. In an attempt to re-kindle his interest, I wore my best, figure-hugging jeans and green mohair jumper, to match the colour of my eyes. My fair hair is as straight and flat as a roll of wallpaper, but I got up early each morning to create a mass of curls round my shoulders.

If Alan had been a hairdresser, maybe he would have reacted. As it was, he seemed to find something far more enticing in the depths of his tub of gloss paint.

As Alan's friendship grew cooler, I found myself thinking about him almost constantly, going over every detail of his face in my mind. His relaxed manner, his flashes of quirky humour, his quiet determination, his high-spirited play with Simon, oh, everything about him attracted me. And we had talked so well together. Surely he couldn't be completely indifferent?

N EXT morning, Sarah mentioned that Alan would be calling round that evening, to discuss decorating ideas with her and Charles, my brother-in-law, for Simon's room. This looked like being my only opportunity to make an impression, but I needed to think — to form a plan of action.

That night, just after eight, I was ringing my sister's door-bell. I knew Alan was there because his van was parked outside.

I'd done my best to look devastating. My favourite grey silk dress always made me look and feel good, and I'd swept up my hair in a sophisticated style. Surely I could arouse a flicker of interest?

Sarah showed me into the living-room, where Charles and Alan were talking animatedly.

"I've called in with Simon's teddy," I said, delivering my carefully-rehearsed lines. "He'd buried it in my bag, and I thought he might need it to go to sleep. Oh, hello, Alan."

"Hello," Alan replied. It was obvious from the look on his face that all my preparations hadn't been in vain. "Going anywhere special?"

"Just for a drink with friends," I lied. "Nothing much."

"Have a lovely time, then." He smiled, turning back to Charles and they resumed their discussion.

Well, that was it. I'd done all I could to attract his attention. Now I had to admit defeat. Whatever it took to land Alan Boon, I hadn't got it.

Next day was Alan's last, and I decided to take Simon out for the day rather than face him.

We went swimming and ate at a café. We were late getting back and I was hoping that Alan would have gone. It would be a relief not to see him today.

His van was still there.

"Enjoy yourself last night?" he asked casually, after he'd said hello to Simon.

"Yes, thank you," I replied in a cool tone. I'd had a dismal evening, but wasn't going to admit it.

"What's your next job?" I inquired, politely.

"A ten-year-old's bedroom." He smiled. "The room's a good shape, but the boy has chosen the paper himself. I'll need sun-glasses to cope with the colours! What about you? Back to college?"

"That's right."

He hesitated, awkwardly, then reached out his hand.

"I suppose this is goodbye then." We shook hands. "I wish you all the luck in the world with your career."

"You, too." I kept my frosty self-control. "I'm sure you'll succeed in your business."

Alan gave Simon a last piggy-back round the room, and he was gone.

BY the time Sarah returned, my cool manner had melted and I was sobbing into a tissue. I didn't feel like going home to my parents and sniffled my way through supper with Sarah and Charles.

"Plenty more fish in the sea, more buses along in a minute," my brother-in-law gabbled, in an unsuccessful effort to cheer me. Like most men he felt uncomfortable in the presence of a sobbing female. After supper Sarah bundled me off to have a warm soothing bath. Feeling calmer after a comforting soak I came down wrapped in one of Charles's old dressing-gowns to help Sarah with the washing-up.

Charles answered the door-bell when it rang. A moment later Alan appeared in the kitchen. I was conscious of my hair dripping down my neck as I stared open-mouthed at him.

"I didn't expect to see you here!" he blurted out, tactlessly.

"I can easily go upstairs if you wish to talk privately," I offered.

"No, no." For once, he seemed lost for words. "I was . . . Actually I was coming to ask your sister for your address."

As Sarah and I gaped at him, he began his explanation, which quaintly, he addressed to Sarah.

"I wanted to ask Laura to come out with me, but didn't feel I could while I was working for you. I wouldn't want anyone to feel I was abusing my position in any way."

"Abusing your position?" Sarah inquired, bemused.

"Well, yes. Laura is much younger than me, and you employed me to decorate, not to use my presence in the house to get to know her."

"I appreciate your — er — delicacy," Sarah said. "Excuse me a moment, I must just go and say something to Charles . . ."

With that less than convincing exit, she left us alone.

★　　　★　　　★　　　★

Misunderstandings can be so marvellous. At least, clearing them up is. One evening some weeks later, when Alan and I were comfortably curled up together on his sofa, I felt confident enough to tackle him about his behaviour.

"You were nothing but a tease, playing with a girl's affections for two solid weeks!"

He laughed.

"I've never had to show such self-restraint! After the first couple of days, I was desperate to ask you out! But I was sure you'd refuse — and that might have spoiled the atmosphere. I really enjoyed being with you and Simon."

"I wouldn't have refused," I reminded him.

"How was I supposed to know that? You came in looking more gorgeous every day, you've got a promising career ahead of you, and you're ten years younger than me . . . I didn't think I'd stand a chance!"

He began to chuckle ruefully, and gave his heart-lurching grin.

"That afternoon, when you came back from swimming, you were so cold and stand-offish — I didn't know what to think. I'm still amazed I had the courage to come back again and risk more frost-bite!"

Well, I'm happy to say the Ice-Age is over — now it's time for a little global warming! □

MARTHA GREIG was lying back against a mound of pillows feeling utterly miserable. She stared at the closed door, wishing that she was in the main ward instead of this tiny, little claustrophobic side room.

She could hear sounds — footsteps, voices, laughter — all tantalisingly muffled, as if to make her feel even more isolated on purpose. She closed her eyes. If only I could sleep, she thought, the hours wouldn't seem so long! I wish someone would just tell me how the operation went. How much longer must I stay in here?

She opened her eyes and blinked hard, determined to trap the tear of self-pity which was trying to escape from the corner of her eye. Yet, for all she couldn't sleep, she finally drifted off.

When she opened her eyes again, she knew she must have slept for quite a while because the room was filled with people — all the doctors and nurses who came in to see her every day just before lunchtime.

"How are you today, Mrs Greig?"

"I'm fine, thank you." She felt foolish and dopey as she looked towards the doctor she thought had spoken to her. She was not quite sure if he was the surgeon who had performed her operation; if so, then he was the person she must ask, like the young nurse had told her earlier on. But they all looked the same in their white coats and they all spoke to her so kindly.

"We'll just have a look at you," he was saying now. While the sister turned back the sheet, he moved away to speak to the other doctors.

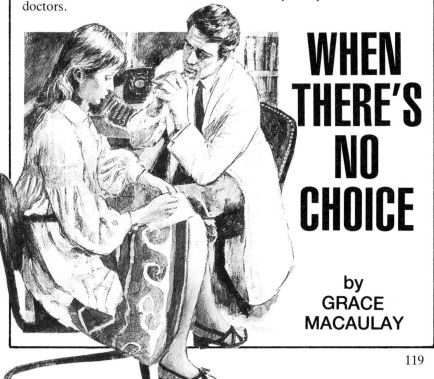

WHEN THERE'S NO CHOICE

by
GRACE
MACAULAY

B UT now Martha had collected her wits, and when he came near her again she was ready with her question.

"Can I go home now?" She added in a firmer voice, "I'm well enough, Doctor."

"All in good time, Mrs Greig," he answered, smiling. "Aren't we treating you properly? Are you not comfortable here?"

"I've never been so well looked after in all my life," she told him promptly, "and I'm very grateful for everything that's been done for me . . ."

But she had lost his attention. He was talking to the other doctors about her case and they were all looking at her tummy and then her charts . . . they seemed to be pleased with her progress. Finally, the surgeon spoke to her as he moved towards the door.

"No fretting to leave us now, Mrs Greig! We'll be sure to send you home very soon."

"Excuse me," Martha interrupted, perhaps a shade too loudly, for he looked mildly surprised. Undeterred, she asked, "Can I talk to you for a minute?"

He nodded and gestured for the others to go out.

Sister Sheila Drummond moved closer to him, blocking his route to the patient.

"Could I have a word with you?" she murmured.

"Certainly, Sister," he said sharply. "If you will be so kind as to wait?"

Sister Drummond stepped aside smartly and joined the others outside the door. She decided to ignore Staff Nurse's whispered remark, "That man can be insufferable without even trying!"

Six months ago, Sister Drummond had congratulated herself on the fact that she and Dr Philip Lewis had kept their romance a secret for almost eight weeks. Privately, Sheila would have liked to keep it that way indefinitely. But unfortunately, Philip had other ideas.

He wanted to marry her. In fact, to her extreme indignation, he took her acceptance for granted. Then, last night, he had told her over dinner that he saw no reason why they should not announce their engagement immediately.

She was still amazed at how peeved he had been when she said she needed time to consider . . .

★   ★   ★   ★

It had become something of a habit for Philip to take coffee in Sheila's office after the ward round. But today, for the first time, she found herself wishing that the tradition didn't exist. She would have preferred not to be alone with him right now.

"I'm sorry if I seemed a bit ungracious." He stirred his coffee, and when Sheila remained silent, he gazed at her with his head tilted and pleaded, "Forgive me?"

She gave a cool shrug. "It doesn't matter."

A tense silence ensued.

"So what was it you wanted to say to me?" Philip asked finally.

When There's No Choice

Sheila looked at his face and a perverse imp of mischief made her tease him.

"Surely you didn't imagine I was going to say, 'Sorry about saying no to you last night — let's make our announcement here in the middle of the ward round'?" She halted, staring at him in amazement — because his face was beaming with pleasure.

"Do you mean that, Sheila?" As she shook her head his smile faded — he looked hurt and perplexed.

"Sarcasm is wasted on you." But Sheila spoke in a small subdued voice, and felt forced to add, "I'm sorry, I suppose I'm on edge. But I said that to try to make you realise that my private life has no connection with my work. I wanted to speak to you about the patient.

"I've had two phone calls from her relatives this morning — one from her husband and one from her daughter — both asking us not to discharge her yet, no matter what she says."

Philip frowned.

"I gather her granddaughter is getting married tomorrow and she is very anxious to be at the wedding."

"You didn't agree — " Sheila looked alarmed.

"Of course not," he snapped, then added apologetically, "We seem to be back to square one, you and me." Looking into her eyes, he told her, "I love you, Sheila, and I thought . . . I believed that you loved me."

"I do." She sighed.

This was neither the time nor the place to repeat her reasons for not wanting to marry. She looked away from his troubled face.

"So what did you say to Mrs Greig? She isn't likely to walk out, is she? She is a very determined lady."

"I think — well, I hope I've made her understand that if she does too much too soon she's going to delay her recovery." He paused and gave Sheila a smile which had the effect of making her heart lurch. "I'm sure my bedside manner has charmed Mrs Greig into realising that her health is more important than missing the wedding."

Sheila smiled back at him and touched his hand.

"You are nice, Philip. And I do love you."

"But . . ." The unspoken question hung in the air between them as he grasped her hand and prompted her to say more. Sheila merely shook her head — she was relieved when the telephone rang and she had to answer it.

IN the side ward, Martha Greig was sitting in a chair by the window when Sister Drummond came to see her, some time later.

"Well, Sister, I made a bid for freedom but I'm afraid you must keep me until I'm better!"

"You'll soon be strong enough to go home," Sheila Drummond told her with a smile. "Your husband and your daughter both called to inquire for you. I told them you had a comfortable night . . . they both send their love."

121

"I told them I'd surely be home today." Mrs Greig sighed. "But they didn't believe me. I would have loved to see Aileen married, but I expect they'll manage without me — and I shall be able to see it all later on the video. David, my youngest son, will be doing the video."

"How many sons do you have?" Sheila Drummond asked. "I've noticed you always have lots of visitors."

"We have four sons, three daughters and nine grandchildren," Mrs Greig replied proudly. "I keep them all in order, you know. Granny Bossy, they call me behind my back!

"I can't imagine any of them getting along without me. I've spent my entire life caring for them all, and sorting out their problems. It's not easy to sit here idle."

"But you aren't absolutely idle," Sheila pointed out. "Your body is busy working to heal itself. A major operation needs a major recovery programme, you know. We can do our part but your own state of mind counts for a lot in the healing process."

Mrs Greig nodded.

"That clever Doctor Lewis said something like that, too!" She smiled. "I promised him faithfully that I shall do everything I'm told. He has a way with him, that one! He makes me feel that he cares for me, as if I'm someone special."

"You *are* special, Mrs Greig. You are our patient, and we want to see you getting fit and well."

It was the sort of conversation Sheila Drummond had been taking part in all her nursing career . . . and yet there was something different today, some significance which she could not quite put her finger on.

A S the day went on, snatches of the conversation kept coming back to her. But the puzzle inside her head remained unsolved — until a few minutes before she went off duty.

It was her custom to go around the ward to exchange a few words with each patient just before she left. Mrs Greig was the last — and Sheila could see at once that the older woman's spirits were low. Yet, in answer to Sister's question about how she was feeling, Mrs Greig managed to smile.

"I'm fine, thank you, Sister — just a bit tired after all my visitors."

"Well, I hope you get a good night's sleep." Sheila spoke with a reassuring smile. "I'll see you in the morning."

But as she went out, Sheila was suddenly and acutely aware of something. That morning, Mrs Greig had admitted that the wedding would go ahead without her. Outwardly, she had been sad, but inwardly she must have been so frustrated at being unable to go because of her illness. She hadn't any say in the matter, really.

Oh dear, Sheila thought. I understand exactly how she feels! I could be in the same boat.

If I marry Philip Lewis and give up my work then this ward, these patients, will be managed perfectly well without me. That Philip! Why didn't he even just ask me what I thought about us getting

Historic Scotland

THE BATTLE OF LARGS
(Bowen Craig Tower)

ANYONE who stood on Bowen Craig, south of Largs, on a stormy day in October 1263, must have witnessed scenes they would never forget.

For on the shore here, now marked by the Round Tower shown in my sketch, took place the Battle of Largs, a turning point in Scottish history.

The reign of Alexander III was mainly peaceful, but at that time King Haakon of Norway looked upon the Scottish Hebrides as outposts of his empire, and diplomacy failed to make him think otherwise.

In fact, Haakon took matters into his own hands, and set sail with the largest fleet that had ever left Norway to settle the Hebridean dispute once and for all by attacking the Scottish mainland.

Diplomacy having failed, Alexander used strategy. He lured Haakon's fleet far from its bases into the trap of the Firth of Clyde, where the ships anchored at Arran. Then he waited.

It was October, and inevitably there came the equinoctial gales. The great Viking fleet was battered and torn from its moorings. Many of the ships were driven helplessly ashore at Largs, where the survivors were easily vanquished.

King Haakon and his remaining ships returned northwards, back to his base in Orkney, and there he took ill and died.

As a result of this, Norway lost its hold of the Hebrides, and they were ceded to Alexander's kingdom.

married! Still, if it's a choice between work and Philip . . .

The night staff were arriving, so it was too late to make a personal phone call from the ward. Sheila had to wait nervously until she was at home in her flat before she rang Philip to tell him.

"My answer is yes, darling. Now that I've said so, I can't think why I hesitated!"

Philip Lewis should have been elated, yet there was a note of caution in his voice.

"We have to talk, Sheila . . . shall we go out for a meal?"

Had he changed his mind? While she showered and dressed, Sheila felt a bit panicky.

It seemed an eternity until Philip arrived. She threw her arms around him and there was no doubt in her mind about her love for him.

"Can I count on this kind of welcome every time we're apart for a few hours?" he asked lightly.

"I hope so," she murmured, and he kissed her tenderly.

She tried to tell him how worried she'd been, and her words tumbled over each other.

"From now on we must promise to trust each other," he said once she'd finished. "Our love is too precious to be wasted by misunderstandings!"

"Agreed!" Sheila smiled.

She went on to tell him more about the chat with Mrs Greig which had disturbed her.

"I felt the same as Mrs Greig," she told him. "She has no choice about missing her granddaughter's wedding. I am so in love with you that I have no choice either! My life would have no meaning without you . . ."

Philip gazed at her solemnly.

"You could still work once we're married — lots of women do. I wouldn't mind."

Sheila shook her head.

"No, not me — I would prefer to be a full-time wife . . . and mother."

"How many children shall we plan for?" Philip asked with a smile.

"Let's wait and see!" Sheila laughed, but soon, she thought of her patient again. "Mrs Greig has four sons, three daughters and nine grandchildren . . . I expect she will have great-grandchildren soon . . ."

MARTHA Greig knew nothing of the part she had played in the ward sister's romance. Everyone saw, though, that the young woman seemed so happy today.

But Sister Sheila Drummond was as alert as always to any unexpected change in a patient's condition, and that evening she spoke to Mrs Greig.

"You are progressing amazingly fast!" She saw the sparkle in the patient's eyes, and asked, "Is there a secret behind your happy smile, tonight, Mrs Greig?"

"Not a secret, not now," Mrs Greig replied mysteriously. She chuckled before she went on. "I thought the wedding was to be today, as you know. Then when my husband came to visit me he was wearing old grey trousers and a tweed jacket, so naturally I began to scold him for going to the wedding looking like a scarecrow!

"Then didn't my daughter, Madge, arrive — not looking at all like the mother of the bride! Being me, I started on at her as well! But before I got going they looked at each other and laughed and said it was clear that I was fit to hear some good news, so Madge went out and in came Aileen — the bride — and her lad!

"What do you think? They've postponed the wedding for two weeks! Our Aileen gave me a great big kiss and told me she wouldn't dream of getting married without me there to see that it was all properly done!" She paused and gave a long blissful sigh.

"It's lovely to feel loved and needed — I just can't tell you how good it feels, Sister."

But Sheila did not need to be told. She knew exactly what Mrs Greig meant. □

by BETTY McINNES

A Granny On Approval

"NOW, you behave your-self, Mrs Munro!"

The warden of Roselea Sheltered Housing Complex wagged a warning finger at the elderly lady sitting demurely in the hallway. The dear old soul looked mortally offended.

"I always behave myself, Warden. I don't get a chance to do otherwise, do I?" she retorted.

The warden ignored the impish gleam in Mrs Munro's blue eyes.

"You know fine what I mean, my dear! I don't have to spell it out to you, do I?" she replied darkly.

Mrs Munro examined her shining shoes and hooked her brolly more firmly over her arm, all to avoid the warden's accusing look.

"I believe in speaking my mind, that's all. What's wrong with telling the truth?" she asked huffily.

"Nothing, so long as you don't start a miniature civil war every time!" The warden shook her head despairingly over the innocent-looking old lady.

The other residents of Rose-lea had grown to appreciate Mrs Munro's many sterling qualities, but everyone knew that if she opened her mouth to pass judgment on someone's new hat, or curtains, or what-ever, they could expect an honest opinion, and if the truth proved unpalatable, that was just too bad!

They'd learned to live with Mrs Munro's uncomfortable honesty, but it had taken time, and there had been heated rows and floods of tears until everyone at Roselea had finally got used to her habit of plain speaking.

"Anyway, I was quite right about Mr Bartholomew's beard," Mrs Munro was saying smugly. "He's had a new lease of life since he shaved it off. It made him look terribly old."

"My dear, he's our oldest resident. Ninety-three and proud of it. He's entitled to look old, if he wants to," the warden protested.

"Well, he doesn't look a day over seventy now. I rather fancy him myself." Mrs Munro smiled wickedly.

The warden hastily dropped the subject. Time was getting on, and Mrs Munro's visitors would be here any minute. The outcome of their visit was of crucial importance to the warden, because she hoped it would result in the old lady's life becoming a little less lonely.

If only Mrs Munro could curb her devastating honesty! She sat down beside her and took her hand, hoping to get the message firmly across to the stubborn old dear.

"Now, remember what I told you, love. Mr and Mrs Barton are ever such a nice young couple, about the same age as your son in Australia and his wife. Mr Barton enjoyed a wonderful relationship with his granny when he was a little boy, and he wants his own little boy to share his experience.

"Unfortunately, both Mr and Mrs Barton's parents are dead, and that's where you come in, Mrs Munro. When they contacted Roselea and offered to adopt a granny, I recommended you. You won't let me down, will you, Mrs Munro?" the warden pleaded.

"Well . . . what are their plans for the afternoon? Do you know?" Mrs Munro asked apprehensively.

"Mr Barton said something about a drive in the country and a picnic, if the weather's fine," the warden answered.

Mrs Munro's eyes misted dreamily.

"Know what I'd like? A walk down the crowded High Street this Saturday afternoon, followed by fish and chips and cream cakes, in a café."

The warden patted her arm tolerantly.

"Crowds of people make you dizzy, love, and your digestion wouldn't stand for fish and chips and cream cakes. It's a lovely afternoon, and a picnic will be fun."

"Just so long as I don't get meat paste sandwiches. Everyone gives us old folk meat paste. It's coming out of my ears!" the old lady grumbled.

The warden held up a hand sternly. "That's enough, Mrs Munro! Remember, you must watch your tongue, or else . . . !"

The unfinished threat hung in the air, but Mrs Munro knew perfectly well what it was. It was lonely days spent without the merry chatter of young ones, and Christmas spent in the company of old folk like herself, with no young bairn to watch as he opened his

126

presents, his wee face glowing. That's why Mrs Munro was feeling so edgy.

She was just as keen as the warden to make a good impression on the young couple and their little boy. She straightened the jaunty tilt of her hat to a more sober angle, as befitted a granny-on-approval.

"I'll do my best, Warden. Can't do more than that, can I?" she said grimly.

NOW, you behave yourself, Kevin!" Dorothy Barton turned round in the passenger seat, the better to fix her young son with a warning glare. The sheltered-housing complex was in sight, and Dorothy knew Kevin was an unwilling participant in this afternoon's excursion. He was football daft, and it had taken hours of patient argument to persuade him to give up his Saturday afternoon playing with his pals in the park.

He shone with unaccustomed cleanliness, hair slicked down, except for the cow's lick at the back, and he was being unusually polite and silent. It made her nervous.

Steven, her husband, was happily reliving the times he'd enjoyed with his granny when he was a boy, and was looking forward immensely to meeting the dear old lady waiting for them at the foot of the tree-lined avenue.

Historic Scotland
THE SOLDIER'S LEAP, Killiecrankie

IN the heart of the deeply wooded Pass of Killiecrankie lies the rocky defile of the River Garry. Where the river struggles most fiercely to free itself from its cage of rocks is The Soldier's Leap.

Leaping across the river at this point was a daring feat made by a soldier named Donald MacBean to avoid capture when General Mackay's army was routed and scattered by an army of Highlanders gathered together by Graham of Claverhouse, Viscount Dundee.

The battle was fought on July 17, 1689, and it was all over in five minutes, for Mackay's army were overwhelmed by the wild charge made by the Highlanders.

Alas, tragedy struck in the moment of "Bonnie Dundee's" victory. A stray shot from his fast-retreating adversaries found its mark, and the leader fell, fatally wounded. A stone marks the spot, about a mile from the head of the Pass.

The Pass of Killiecrankie is in the care of the National Trust for Scotland, and nearby there is an Information Centre.

The walk through the Pass is picturesque at all seasons.

"You wait till you meet your new granny, Kevin! Grannies are special people, you know. They have time. They'll listen to all your troubles. You're lucky this dear lady has agreed to do the job!" he said.

"I'd rather have a new football!" Kevin muttered, but he kept his voice down, wisely. His mother had sharper ears than Kenny Dalglish, Kevin's Jack Russell terrier. She whipped round, frowning suspiciously.

"What did you say?"

"I said, d'you think the granny could play football?" he replied innocently, a good piece of defensive strategy, because it made them laugh.

"Darling, Mrs Munro's an elderly lady. I don't think she'll be interested in football," his mother said. She turned away and left him to his own thoughts.

Not interested in football! That was a disappointment.

When the granny idea was first mentioned some weeks ago, Kevin had been quite enthusiastic. His training sessions in the back garden were sadly hampered by the absence of someone to play on the wing. His little dog, Kenny Dalglish, made a reasonable goalie despite his tendency to sink his fangs into the ball. Kevin was striker, of course, but someone on the wing would improve his passing skills no end. He'd hoped the new granny would be nippy on her feet, and plug the gap.

"Oh dear, I hope she likes us!" his mother said anxiously as they drew up outside the pleasant complex of small houses and apartments at the end of the avenue.

"You leave everything to me, love!" his father reassured her. "I know what grannies like. I'm an expert!"

Kevin and his mother remained in the car, and presently Steven Barton emerged proudly with a neat, elderly lady hanging on to his arm.

Kevin thought the granny didn't look very happy. In fact, she looked just like he felt, apprehensive and nervous. There was a flurry of talk and introductions, then the tidy, little lady was seated beside him in the back seat. They smiled at one another warily.

"Off we go then!" his father cried jovially.

Mrs Munro ventured a sideways glance at the solemn, little boy. He was very clean and tidy, and not a bit like that other little boy she remembered so vividly, her son Jack, now grown up and married, and living in Australia. My, what a grubby, little rascal he had been! The washing and ironing she'd had, to keep him looking half decent! He'd kept her busy, every day.

She supposed wee boys must be different nowadays, always sitting indoors, goggling at television. It seemed a pity. She couldn't think of anything to say to this silent, tidy, little boy.

Kevin studied the granny covertly. She was quite sturdy, her feet encased in sensible shoes which could deliver a good kick, but by no stretch of the imagination could he see her as a speedy right winger.

THE LITTLE BLACK SNOWMAN

*T*HE shop was bright with festive gifts,
　As far as the eye could see,
Games and books and toys and sweets,
　Decorations for the tree.

There was a box of silver snowmen,
　Shimmering and sparkling and bright,
Except for one, which was almost black,
　Without a glint of light.

He knew no-one would want him
　Hanging on their tree,
That he'd stay for ever in the box,
　He could almost guarantee.

He was all alone on Christmas Eve,
　Of being bought he had no hope,
When someone shook the snowmen box,
　And hands began to grope.

And so the little black snowman
　Went home with Isadore,
Who hung him on her tree with joy
　That year and many more.

That he was dark and almost black,
　She didn't really mind,
It's the shape and feel that matter,
　To a little girl who's blind.

— Joan Coatswith.

"A mystery tour, eh, Mrs Munro?" his father was saying.

Kevin watched the granny peer suspiciously at the passing country-side, open her mouth as if to say something, then close it again.

"Very nice, I'm sure!" she said in a careful, little voice.

It wasn't really a mystery tour, because Kevin knew where they were going. His parents had argued endlessly about it, and in the end they'd both agreed on the Redcastle picnic area. It was a lovely place, with wooden tables and chairs and a sheltering roof over the top, set amongst trees and bushes and parkland.

Kevin usually loved going there, but he didn't view the outing with any enthusiasm today. He'd been forbidden to bring his football, and Kenny had been firmly banished to his kennel, until they found out if the granny liked dogs or not.

"Here we are!" Steven Barton stopped the car in the car park with a flourish. It was a lovely day, the sky blue, and dotted with whipped-cream clouds, and the grass a fresh green. This was just the sort of outing his own dear gran had enjoyed.

He and Dorothy helped Mrs Munro out of the car and seated her tenderly in the picnic area. She seemed rather subdued, Steven thought, but maybe she was just enjoying the fresh air and peace. It must be a rare treat for her. He signalled Kevin to sit down.

Kevin's behaviour had been exemplary, and he was so clean and tidy, Steven hardly recognised him. He withdrew tactfully to help his wife with the picnic basket, leaving Kevin and Mrs Munro alone together.

Mrs Munro had braced herself stoically for the cold wind that was sure to strike, sooner or later. Nasty, draughty place, the countryside! This was a sheltered spot, though, and she soon relaxed, drowsily enjoying the sunshine.

Kevin swung his legs and daydreamed about the game of football he should be playing. He'd have to train extra hard next week, or he'd lose his place in the team. Pity this granny couldn't run. That would have helped a lot, he thought.

"Steven, they're awfully quiet!" Dorothy Barton whispered anxiously, studying the two silent figures on the bench.

"I expect they're wondering when the food will arrive. You know what our Kevin's appetite is like!" Steven grinned, lifting the hamper out of the boot.

Dorothy laid a brightly-checked cloth on the table and diffidently set the food out before their guest.

"These are egg sandwiches, Mrs Munro, and those are pâté and salad."

"Pâté? Isn't that posh meat paste?" Mrs Munro interrupted suspiciously, and the young couple laughed. Even Kevin smiled.

"Yes, I made it myself." Dorothy smiled proudly, and Mrs Munro didn't have the heart to say anything. She took a cautious bite.

"Why, it's lovely!" she answered with relief, and settled down to sample everything with relish.

A Granny On Approval

WHEN the picnic was over and the table cleared, Steven had another little treat in store. He took Mrs Munro's arm and set off along the path through the woods, Kevin trailing along behind.

"I'm going to show you one of the best views in Scotland, Mrs Munro. My dear old gran used to love it!" Steven told her nostalgically.

They came out of the wood, and there was the strath spread out before them, with the lovely, blue mountains beyond. It was a bonnie view, but Mrs Munro's eyes fastened at once upon the washing flapping in the breeze in the garden of a nearby cottage.

Oh, what a lovely washing, she thought appreciatively. There were sparkling white sheets billowing in the wind, and a row of shirts tugging and dancing on the line. Towels and socks, pants and dungarees, waved bravely like pennants in the wind.

It reminded Mrs Munro of her own proud washing days, when her husband was alive and her son was young, and every hour of the day was busy, happy and fulfilled. A tear formed in her eye, then another.

"Oh, how beautiful!" she whispered softly.

"I knew you'd like it!" Steven's chest swelled proudly.

Kevin had been watching the granny curiously. She wasn't looking at Dad's old mountains, her eyes were fastened on a washing just like his mum's, in the cottage garden. It occurred to Kevin suddenly that it must be a sad day for an old mum, when she didn't have washing to do any more.

His mother grumbled about the heaps of washing he gave her, with football strips and all that, but he'd noted the proud look on her face when it was all done and hanging on the line, dazzling clean.

He felt very sorry for Mrs Munro, who'd nobody's washing to do. Tentatively, he tugged at her jacket, looking up at her.

"You could come and do my mum's ironing, if you like. She hates ironing," Kevin suggested. He and Mrs Munro stared at one another, ignoring his mother's outraged squeal of protest.

He understands, Mrs Munro thought, her heart lifting. Why, this is a grand, little lad, just like my Jack! He knows a granny likes to feel useful, and needed. She smiled at him gently.

"I'd like that, Kevin." She nodded.

Kevin was swiftly rearranging his training sessions. If he put the doggy Kenny Dalglish on the wing and put his granny in goal, she'd be jolly useful with those stout shoes and that brolly, he thought. He slipped his hand into hers and felt her fingers curl comfortingly round his.

"Gran, d'you think you could learn to play football?" Kevin asked.

His new granny, ally, accomplice and friend felt a renewed glow of health and vigour, a fresh confidence in the future. She beamed at him.

"Son, I'll tackle anything!" she promised. □

For Ever True

ALMOST a week had passed without Mum
or myself mentioning Aunt Meg.

It wasn't easy. I knew Mum was trying to
keep me from fretting, while I was
anxious not to stir the pain she was feeling at the loss
of her older and only sister.

I caught glimpses of this sorrow when Mum glanced
at the lovely smiling face in the large photograph
above our living-room fireplace.

Aunt Meg had been like a second mum to me. Her
cosy little cottage had been my second home, where I
had built up a store of happy, wonderful memories.

Even now I could recall the inviting aroma of her
baking that had always greeted our arrival for a
weekend stay. And how could I ever forget the
warm, safe feeling I had as a child as she tucked me
into the little bed in my very own spare room?

Perhaps strongest of all was the memory of stretch-
ing out on the rug before her open fire, its heat
reddening my cheeks.

I could still see Aunt Meg's face smiling down at
me. "You watch you don't melt there, my dear,"
she'd tease me.

When I was young I used to urge Aunt Meg to tell
me about her experiences in the war. To a girl of six
and seven they seemed exciting, and I pored over her
old album with photographs of her and other smiling
young women in their smart ATS uniforms.

I hadn't quite accepted her death, but the blessing
was that it had been sudden and quick. Doctor Brent
had told us that her heart had just given up.

by
CATHIE
MITCHELL

There was also comfort in knowing she had led a full and active life. The numbers who came to her funeral were testimony to the many lives she had touched.

The church youth organisations, smart and shining in their uniforms, had been there. The Woman's Guild members, mothers and fathers who remembered the gentle little woman who'd been their Sunday school teacher and, of course, older friends from the Senior Citizens' club were all present, sharing the loss with us.

I remember musing over the oddity of Aunt Meg in the ATS. It clashed with this kind, patient figure, for ever ready with a gentle word or a welcoming smile. But, of course, the war was a long time ago. Even Mum had been in the ATS and she had the same soft nature!

Dad had seen to the painful disposal of the cottage and its many treasures. Mum took a few things, just as reminders. But for myself, the old photo album was enough.

However, for months I could not bring myself to open it. The pain was still too strong . . .

Dad was right about time being a healer. Gradually, we were able to talk openly about Aunt Meg. We could even recount amusing incidents and laugh a little.

I suppose it was inevitable that I would again think the thought that had sometimes arisen in my mind over the years. Why had Aunt Meg never married?

I had put the question to Mum on several occasions, but she always shrugged it off with a vague, "Who knows?"

Sometimes I had pressed her. "Aunt Meg would have made a wonderful mother. She's such a caring person," I used to tell her.

Mum agreed, of course, but that was it.

"And she was such a lovely girl," I would persist. "You only have to look at her old photographs — she looked great in her uniform. I think she must've turned a few heads when she was young."

Mum always ended the discussion by suddenly remembering something she had to do.

WITH the passing of time, I was able to think again of how I had felt that there was something missing in Aunt Meg's life.

I always had the feeling that she kept herself constantly occupied to shut out a disappointment or hurt from the past.

It was during one of our usual family nights at home that I made the discovery. Dad was asleep in his chair, the newspaper sagging on his lap. Mum was knitting, facing him across the fire. I was flicking through a magazine . . .

I still don't know what prompted me to fetch Aunt Meg's old photo album from my room.

Mum looked up as I returned, her eyes darting to the album, then back at me. For an instant I thought she was going to say something, then her attention returned to the pattern that was resting on her lap.

I turned the pages casually, having scanned the album many times over the years. I could probably have described every photograph by heart.

Finally, with a sigh, I made to close it when I spotted a tiny corner of white just inside the back cover. I tugged at the white triangle and to my astonishment, pulled out a photograph.

"Mum. Look at this!" I couldn't hide my excitement — was this the missing link I'd been searching for all these years?

The picture was of Aunt Meg, like many of the others, in her ATS uniform. But this time there was a man standing beside her with one arm across her shoulders. He was tall, strikingly handsome and wearing Army uniform. There was a small, hump-like, stone bridge in the background.

"What is it, dear?" Mum asked, breaking into my thoughts.

"It's Aunt Meg, but there's a man with her — a soldier."

I was surprised by how quickly Mum came to me and almost snatched the photograph from my hand. I looked at her, puzzled by the tearful expression on her face.

"Do you know who he is?" I asked.

"Someone your Aunt Meg met during the war, dear." Mum sighed heavily, handed back the photo and returned to her chair, dabbing her eyes. "Where did you find that?"

"It was tucked into this pocket at the back of the album. I would never have noticed it if it hadn't been sticking out a little."

I could see why I hadn't discovered the almost secret pocket before now. The last three pages of the album were blank, so I never actually turned them.

Had I not been turning all the pages idly, dreamily, the hidden photo would have remained where it had clearly been for years.

"Who is the man?" I persisted. Clearly, if Aunt Meg had kept the picture all these years, it must have meant a lot to her.

"Look at the back," Mum said quietly, nodding to the picture.

I did. The ink was still clear, the words brief but meaningful.

We will meet here again, when it is all over. Love for ever — Tom.

"Tom Findlay was his name," Mum said. "They met during the war."

She swallowed before going on. "I suppose there's no harm in telling you her secret now. I never met him myself, but Meg told me a lot about him. They were very much in love, you know."

"That's why she never married!"

I almost shouted the words and caused Dad to stir, mumble something, then go back to sleep.

"Was he killed in the war?"

Mum sighed again. "He must have been — Meg never saw him again."

"Didn't they write to each other?"

"Of course, for months. Then when Meg was posted south, she kept writing. But suddenly, his letters stopped and after that there was nothing . . . " Her voice trailed away wistfully.

We sat in silence for a long time. Somehow neither of us felt we could find words to justify the unfairness of it all.

It was a simple story that was probably repeated countless times during the war. Two young people thrown suddenly together, falling in love then losing touch in the maelstrom that was raging around them at that time.

Now I knew I'd been right. There had been a gap, a longing in Aunt Meg's life. I had sensed it, but I'd never realised how deep it actually was. How was I even to guess that she had lost her one true love?

Hearing something tap faintly on the photograph in my hand, I looked down and saw my tear spreading across it. Anxiously, I brushed it clean. Nothing must damage this precious picture, not after all those years . . .

For weeks I was haunted by the photograph. I carried it in my handbag and looked at it at every opportunity. I almost felt privileged to observe Aunt Meg and Tom Findlay smiling back at me with all the gaiety and happiness of true love.

Mum told me the full story, even how she and Aunt Meg had gone once to the bridge after the war.

"I told her it was pointless," Mum told me knowingly. "But she wanted to see the place again. I think she had to. After that she never went back. She couldn't wait there for ever in the hope that by some miracle Tom had survived the war and would come back, too."

That was when I decided to go. I had a few days off and I could be there in three hours.

It was a long drive, but the urge to see the old bridge was too strong. Somehow I needed to see it, to complete my memories of dear Aunt Meg.

Mum wanted to go with me, but I felt the need to do it alone.

THE bridge was just as it was in the photograph. Only now, isolated from the new road, it lay unused and neglected. I had to walk the length of a field to reach it.

For a long time I stood on the bridge, running my fingers over the rough, worn stones and thinking of how often Aunt Meg and Tom Findlay must have stood in the very same spot, laughing and talking of their hopes for a brighter, happier future . . .

The sound of a man's heavy tread brought me sharply back to the present.

He was very old, wearing an old jacket and heavy boots. His leathery face was clear evidence of his outdoor life. I presumed he was a local farmer.

" 'Morning, miss." He touched his battered hat with a flash of courtesy that was as faded as the colour of his jacket. "Lovely day for a walk!"

"Yes, it is," I replied politely. I was conscious of his penetrating gaze studying me intensely and I gave an embarrassed laugh. "I just came here to remember something, or rather someone who used to come here. A long time ago, of course."

"Must have been," he grunted. "Don't get many stopping here now, not since they closed it off and built that new bridge. Don't look much now, I suppose, but it carried a lot of traffic during the war — mainly Army trucks."

He pointed his walking stick into the distance. "There was an Army camp over there, but that has also gone, just like everything else." He looked forlornly towards the ground.

"Were you living here at that time?" I asked, breaking into his thoughts.

"All my days, lass." He paused and I could sense his curiosity. "You're much too young to remember the war, though." ·

I nodded. "Someone I knew, someone very close to me, used to come here then. She was stationed at that camp you were telling me about."

"Really?" He shuffled closer, his eyes roaming affectionately over the tranquil scene.

"I expect this bridge holds memories for a lot who were stationed there. I saw them come here many a time." Then he smiled. "Couples mostly!"

But suddenly he paused and scratched his rough chin. "I'll always remember the fellow who came here — years ago, it was — just like you."

His words struck me like an electric shock. "When was this?" I asked rather harshly.

"Oh, goodness me, a long time ago. Before you were even born I should think!"

"Did he ever come back?" I couldn't hide the tremor in my voice. Was my imagination running wild? It couldn't be! "He didn't say his name by any chance?"

"He didn't say much at all," he told me wistfully. "And if he did come back I never saw him. The only reason I remember him at all was 'cos he showed me this."

His thick fingers ran gently over the rough parapet, lightly brushing away a layer of dust to reveal letters scratched into the stone.

My heart was pounding as I edged closer to look. They had faded, worn by the years of pounding wind and rain, but I could still read them . . .

Meg and Tom. Love for ever.

"So he did come back!" A tide of happiness swept over me.

"What was that, miss?" He looked at me quickly, startled. "Who came back?"

I had to fight hard to keep back the tears, but my heart was singing. The years may have cruelly separated Tom and Aunt Meg, but their love had remained alive, as surely as inscribed on the rough stone.

If there was justice, if there was right at all, Aunt Meg and Tom Findlay were together at last. I had to believe that . . . □

THE back garden was exactly as Evelyn remembered it. Keeping in the shadows, she crept forward, peering through the dusk at the magnolia's beautiful, pink-tipped flowers.

Many times over the years, she had longed to see the tree in full bloom once more. Now, just looking at it reminded her of happier times and eased the loneliness she felt.

Yet, when she'd set off for a walk, earlier this evening, it had certainly not been her intention to return to her old home. She couldn't understand why she felt she had to come here, but here she was.

Evelyn barely noticed the soft breeze that ruffled her silver hair, for a faraway look had come into her blue eyes. Memories of the day when Sam, her husband, had planted the magnolia came flooding back . . .

A TROUBLE SHARED

The children were racing round the lawn. A young girl, with pigtails flying, was being chased by two small, cheeky-faced boys. At their heels a big black dog barked excitedly.

Evelyn gave a tiny sigh. Then her heart fluttered.

Sam was there, too. He was tall, dark and absurdly young, wearing his favourite old, brown polo-neck sweater; the one that matched his eyes. Laughing and teasing as always, he was hiding something behind his back.

"Happy anniversary, darling," he said, revealing a little sapling. "Here's that magnolia you've been hankering after." His lips met hers as they shared a gentle kiss.

Afraid that they were missing something, the children stopped running and closed in on them.

Sam grinned ruefully and winked. From his pocket he drew out his pipe and lit up. He stood for a while watching the smoke curl towards the sky. Then he scanned the garden.

"Where shall I plant it?" Sam picked up his garden fork and paced around. Every few seconds he stopped to look back at Evelyn.

by JANET BOND

Finally he found a spot that satisfied him. "What about here?"

"Perfect," she replied happily.

Instinctively she grabbed hold of the boys just as they were about to dart forward to "help." She crouched down hugging her small sons towards her.

"The best way you three can help —" she glanced sideways at her daughter " — is by giving the little tree some respect and letting it grow in peace."

A S the memory faded, a nostalgic smile hovered on Evelyn's lips. Long after the children had grown up and left home the tree had continued to give her and Sam pleasure. How she'd hated leaving it behind when they moved.

"Too big to transplant, my love," Sam had said slipping his arm round her waist. "Besides, it belongs here. Leave it for the next family to enjoy . . ."

His words were still echoing through Evelyn's mind when suddenly she heard a clicking sound. Realising too late that the back door had opened, she found herself trapped in a rectangular patch of light.

From behind her came a loud gasp.

"Who's there? What are you doing in my garden?"

Evelyn's hand flew to her chest in an effort to still her thumping heart. Slowly she turned.

Her gaze swept fleetingly over the gleaming white walls and dimpled windows of the house before coming to rest on a young woman.

"You nearly frightened the life out of me." The figure framed in the lighted doorway was slight with long fair hair. "What are you doing here?" she demanded again.

"I . . . I'm so sorry," stammered Evelyn, her cheeks flaming. "I didn't mean to scare you. My name's Evelyn Baker . . . I used to live here . . . I just wanted to see the magnolia . . ." Even to herself the words sounded ridiculous.

"At this time of night?" The girl's tone was puzzled.

Drawing nearer, Evelyn observed the young woman's ashen complexion. Judging from the look of her red-rimmed eyes, she'd been crying recently.

Evelyn bit back the questions forming on her lips.

"Let me try to explain," she started again. "You see, my husband, Sam, planted that tree on our tenth wedding anniversary and . . ."

"You should be at home," interrupted the young woman, her voice kinder now. She caught hold of Evelyn's arm, guiding her gently towards the back door. "Come inside for a minute and I'll call a taxi for you."

U NABLE to resist the temptation to see inside, Evelyn gave a little shrug of acceptance. "Thank you, Mrs . . . "

"Morton . . . Joanne."

"I always loved this big kitchen." Evelyn gazed round wistfully.

"Though of course it's a lot different from when I lived here." She ran her hand along the smooth pine of the table, noticing how perfectly it matched the fitted units.

"Compared to this the one I have now is more like a cupboard." Her laugh was hollow. "After my husband died, I moved into one of those purpose-built flats in Reigate Road."

The last traces of Joanne's wary expression disappeared and her features eased into a smile.

"Would you like a cup of tea?" she said suddenly, switching on the kettle as she spoke.

Before answering, Evelyn glanced towards the open door to her left from where she could hear the sound of a television.

"I wouldn't want to disturb your husband."

"He's not here." Joanne's bottom lip trembled.

"In that case, I'd love a cup," Evelyn said gratefully.

"Come through to the sitting-room." Joanne invited, leading the way.

Evelyn followed.

"It's beautiful!" She halted in the doorway. "You've certainly made the most of it." Her gaze swept over the room approvingly.

Evelyn clapped her hand to her mouth. "You must think me very rude, staring like that. It's just that having once lived here . . ."

"I understand." Joanne moved towards the television. As she turned it off her attention was caught by something on the floor.

"Kids!" She rolled her grey eyes heavenward and bent down to retrieve a fluffy blue rabbit from under the coffee table.

"How many children have you?" Evelyn sank down on to the settee and loosened her coat.

"Three." Joanne lifted a framed pastel drawing from the wall and handed it to the older woman. "Two boys and a girl."

"Snap." Evelyn's eyes twinkled as she stared down at the three mischievous little faces. It gave her immense pleasure to think of them playing where once her own children had played.

"Well, just be glad yours aren't all under five." Joanne added with a wry grin, "I'll be glad when mine are grown up."

"Don't say that, my dear," chided Evelyn softly.

"They grow so quickly and before you know it they're gone." Her eyes clouded as she passed back the picture. "Take my three . . . All living in different parts of the country . . ." She suppressed a sigh. "Of course I visit them quite often. My daughter has even suggested that I move nearer to her but . . ." She paused hunching her shoulders. "I couldn't leave here."

There was silence for a moment.

"I didn't really mean what I said about them growing up." Joanne's eyelids drooped. "It's just that I'm going through a difficult time."

When she looked up her eyes were brimming with tears. Her voice broke and she fished in her pocket for a hanky. "The kettle will be ready, I'll go and make the tea."

The Farmer And His Wife

by John Taylor

You can find some of Anne's recipes on pages 152/153

G RANNY — I must call Anne Granny in this case — was worried. I wasn't, just amused.

Did her mother worry so much when Anne took me into her family for the first time? I know she didn't.

I was meant to take them as they were, a very homely, God-loving family, and I did.

"That was different," Anne argued.

Let me explain.

Our eldest grandson was bringing his girlfriend for an evening meal for the first time.

Granny was delighted, but didn't want to let him down.

How could she, I pointed out, if she just acted normally?

"But what will she think of us eating off the wooden table in the kitchen?"

It's a beautiful refectory table, one I'm proud of.

"Shall I set up the meal in the dining-room?" Anne persisted.

"Not likely!" I retorted.

That would make the occasion far too formal in my opinion.

"Well, how can I hide this table?"

I ask you, hide an antique refectory table!

"Use one of those crocheted table-cloths your granny gave us."

B Y the time she returned with the tea-tray, Joanne had recovered her composure.

"Shall I be mother?" she said forcing a weak grin.

Evelyn was curious but she didn't probe. Instead, over their cups of tea, she took the opportunity to explain in full her strong desire to see the magnolia tree and the memories it evoked.

"Sam and I were very close," she confided. "I know it sounds daft, but sometimes I get this feeling that he's . . ." She lowered her eyes. "He's still here, with me, guiding me . . ."

Despite the difference in their ages, the conversation flowed easily and soon they were swapping, as all mothers do, favourite stories about their children.

★   ★   ★   ★

Later, Evelyn inclined her head towards Joanne's wedding photograph.

"Is your husband away on business?" she inquired tentatively.

Immediately she regretted asking, for Joanne's face crumpled and this time her tears were uncontrollable.

She endeavoured to brush them away with the back of her hand and struggling to hold her voice steady, answered, "No. Derek's in hospital.

142

"Which crockery shall I use?" Anne went on.

"Just use the set you bring out when the family comes," I said in exasperation.

It had been bought by Anne in a January sale St Andrews.

When she arrived home with it, I asked why — I knew we didn't need it.

"It's for the first of the boys to get married. It was in the sale."

The first bit was the excuse, the second because Anne cannot resist a bargain.

I'm afraid I don't think something, however cheap it is, is a bargain unless it's something you need!

I WAS brought back to today's problem with Anne asking, "What shall I give them?"

"Them," was grandson and girlfriend.

"Darling, just make it a simple meal or you'll frighten the poor lass into thinking we live as we don't. Two boiled eggs and a sweet!"

If you had seen the look Anne gave me, I should have turned into a pillar of salt.

I won't bore you with the details of the meal which we ate at the kitchen table.

It was a happy meal, and Gran took to the lassie. To be honest, I gave the lad full marks — I felt he'd picked a winner. I guessed she knew how to wash up, bake and keep a home.

I had to smile, two days later when a wee note arrived: "Thank you for a beautiful meal and oh, I loved your kitchen."

The lassie knew to keep sweet with my dear Anne!

"He was badly hurt and it was touch and go for days. I really thought we were going to lose him."

"I'm so sorry, my dear." Evelyn reached out to pat Joanne's hand. "What happened?"

"There was an accident. Someone pulled out of a side road without looking." Still sobbing, she breathed in deeply. "It's been so difficult getting in to see him . . ." She twisted her wedding ring back and forth. "And he's likely to be there for ages yet."

"Don't you have parents or in-laws?"

"Ye — es I do," Joanne answered reservedly. "Derek's father is a widower, but he has a business to run and he likes to visit Derek as much as possible, too."

"What about your parents?" Evelyn leaned forward.

"They live abroad," replied Joanne briskly. "Dad doesn't keep too well, though, and I'd rather not worry them unless I have to.

"Of course, our friends have rallied round to look after the children, but most of them have families of their own . . ." She broke off abruptly.

"I'm sorry," she said, rising. "I shouldn't be worrying you with my troubles. Shall I ring for your taxi now?"

"Please." Evelyn watched thoughtfully as Joanne crossed the room to the telephone. Sitting here in her old home, thinking over Joanne's sad story, it seemed to Evelyn that Sam was very near. She was also sure that he would approve of the suggestion she was about to make.

"The taxi'll be here in a few minutes." Stifling a yawn, Joanne squinted at her wristwatch. "I'm sorry if I've kept you talking too late."

"Not at all. I've enjoyed our chat." Evelyn smiled. "In fact, I know this sounds silly . . ." She paused. ". . . But I'm convinced this was meant to be. Don't you see?" She glanced swiftly at Joanne's puzzled expression, "I could help you. Once I get to know your children, I can babysit any time you want to go to the hospital."

Joanne's face lit up although her response was guarded. "They're a handful, you know."

Evelyn stood up and buttoned her coat.

"Well, we can give it a try."

"Can you really spare the time?" Joanne asked excitedly.

"Bless you!" Evelyn chuckled. "I've all the time in the world."

I'M off to the hospital now," said Joanne, one sunny afternoon a couple of weeks later. She kissed each of the children in turn, reminding them, "Be good."

As they scampered away down the garden she smiled at the elderly woman lounging in a deckchair. "I don't know what I'd, what *we'd*, have done without you, Evelyn."

"My pleasure. I'm so glad that Derek is making good progress." Then her brow furrowed and her voice shook slightly. "Though when he comes home, I shall miss you and the children dreadfully."

"What do you mean?"

"Well." Evelyn's voice dropped. "You won't need me any more."

There was a moment's silence while the two women regarded each other.

"The children have taken to you so well — I had hoped," Joanne ventured, "that when Derek's fully recovered, you would still come round. The children love having you here and so do I." She took Evelyn's hand in hers. "You'll always be welcome here. We want you to look upon our home . . ." She waved her hand round airily. "As if it were your own."

★　　　★　　　★　　　★

As if it were your own. The words repeated themselves over and over again in Evelyn's mind as she looked first at the house, then up at the fading flowers of the magnolia tree and lastly at the children.

Watching them through half-closed eyes, it was so easy to pretend that she'd gone back in time and that they were her own three children romping on the lawn.

Momentarily, she even fancied that she could see her beloved Sam puffing away on his pipe whilst he pottered amongst the plants.

Coming to her senses, she sat upright, shook her head and opened her eyes wide. It was, she reminded herself, all in her imagination.

Perhaps? But, she asked herself, where did that lovely, rich aroma of pipe tobacco come from? □

Love Is All That Matters

by LAURA CALDWELL

IT was Friday lunchtime when Jock McLean broke the news to his wife.

It had been an ordinary day up till then. Kirsty had been at her mother's that morning — as she did every Friday — to have a blether over a cup of tea.

"See you all on Sunday," her mother called as Kirsty left to pick up Jamie from school.

As if she'd forget! Sunday was the day the whole family got together — Mum and Dad, Gran and Grandpa. Kirsty's sister, Dolly, would come along with her husband, Angus, and daughter, Heather. Even old Aunt Lily would be there, tucking into her high tea.

Kirsty hurried down the brae to the school. As it was his first year at school he only had to go in the mornings.

"Well, how was it today, son?"

"Better. We had paints and made a terrible mess, but Mrs Low didn't mind. I made this for you —" He thrust a large square of paper into his mum's hands.

There were splashes of brilliant colour. "Oh, it's — beautiful — it's just — " she was stuck for words.

K   145

"What is it then, Mummy? Say what it is."

"Well — it's a — sunset, isn't it?"

"No, it isn't. You've got it upside down, silly. It goes that way. It's a ship, an enormous ship with red and blue and orange sails . . . and that's the ocean. See now?"

"Of course. A big ship. We'll keep it for Daddy to see."

Kirsty and Jock had been happily married for seven years and enjoyed living in their new council house in Lochie Avenue near to Kirsty's mum. Jock worked for a branch of a national company making surgical instruments. They were content. Jock's job was steady and they had enough money for their needs.

Jamie and his mum had a bowl of soup and a cheese roll each. In the evening, when Jock came home, the three would have a real dinner — mince or lamb hot-pot or maybe a delicious smoked-haddock-and-tattie pie.

Kirsty was a good cook, just like her mother and her granny before her. She turned out dark, treacly gingerbreads, iced fairycakes and tasty cheese scones, too.

In the afternoon Kirsty planned to take Jamie on the bus to Inverness, to the shops to buy him some new clothes.

But that Friday she and Jamie never got into town. Just as they were ready to leave, the front door opened and Jock walked in.

Kirsty was astonished.

"Jock! What is it?" she exclaimed as she noticed his shocked face.

"Jamie, Andy's out there on his bike." Her husband turned to the little boy. "He was asking if you were coming out. Away you go and get some fresh air."

Jamie was all too glad to escape the trip to town. He hauled his bike from the porch and rushed off.

Kirsty was still staring speechlessly at her husband's face. He couldn't meet her eyes.

"The factory is closing, Kirsty!" he said abruptly.

"Oh no —" Kirsty breathed in anguish.

She couldn't think what else to say — her mind was in a whirl. Tryce was part of Kirkmossie!

It was a very small firm, just a wee branch of the giant national company — but her Jock and some of his pals had worked there since leaving school! As their fathers before them . . . Tryce would never close!

"They might have warned you, Jock!"

"Aye — well. They have. I must be honest. Things have been dodgy for a while. I never told you. I convinced myself it couldn't happen . . .

"I'll get some redundancy money, Kirsty. But what's that? I'm young. It's work I want."

Poor Jock. Suddenly Kirsty knew how badly her husband needed her support. She went to put her arms about him.

"You'll find another job. You're clever — you're skilled!"

"Can't you see? I've been trained to do special work. Where else near here takes on surgical instrument makers?"

That night, when Jamie had gone to bed, they discussed the situation further.

"The big bosses — up from the south — had us all into the office at midday," Jock told her. "They explained it was no longer worth the company's while to keep the Kirkmossie works going. It's to close down in August!"

THE whole family was stunned. Kirsty felt a twinge of envy for her sister, Dolly. Angus had his own joiner's business in the village. There would always be work for a good joiner.

Kirsty could hardly sleep for the thoughts and plans racing around inside her head. What would they do? What could they do?

She supposed they could use Jock's redundancy money to open up a wee baker's shop . . . gingerbreads, butterfly cakes, sultana scones. But — she had to face it — Kirkmossie folk didn't need a baker's shop. The housewives did their own baking or brought home fancy cakes from Inverness.

Jock returned home one evening a week later, his brown eyes shining.

"Guess what, darling?"

He lifted her high and twirled her round and round.

"I've got a job! A smashing job!"

She stared in wonder, her mouth open.

"I knew it, I knew it. You'll never lack work, Jock McLean!" She cuddled close to him.

But Jock stayed still and silent. Kirsty stepped back and looked up into his face.

"There's a snag —" He stopped and took a deep breath. "It . . . it isn't in Kirkmossie. It's away a bit —"

"Where? Inverness? But that doesn't matter. You've your motor-bike."

"Not Inverness, Kirsty." He took another deep breath. "Birmingham."

For a moment Kirsty was stunned into silence.

"Bir-ming-ham!" Then she laughed. "You're joking, Jock! You gave me such a fright there. I really believed —"

"But it is true," he cut in sharply. "It's Birmingham. Well, near enough anyway — a few miles south. Where the main factory is. I've been offered the same work there. But with more money, Kirsty . . . to make it worth my while moving."

Kirsty was devastated.

So was her family when they heard the news.

★　　　★　　　★　　　★

As the days went on and the time to leave drew closer, Kirsty seemed incapable of seeing the move in a sensible light. In her mounting anxiety she took it out on Jock.

"You're asking me to leave all my family and the only home I've

147

ever known. You're asking Jamie to leave his school and his grandparents and aunties . . ."

Poor Jock was sorely troubled by Kirsty's attitude. His own parents lived in Fort William and, of course, he was sorry he wouldn't be seeing so much of them but surely the move made sense?

When it came down to choosing between a job or joining the queues of unemployed, there was no choice! Kirsty would have to face facts. They had to move!

Kirsty's heart sank when she first set eyes on their new home. They'd been given a terraced house on Plumgate's new estate. It had a nice garden and a sparkling new kitchen and every labour-saving device a woman could want.

"We're very lucky," Jock reminded his wife.

But in the weeks that followed, his wife grew more and more homesick and pined for her family and the comfortable familiarity of Kirkmossie. Kirsty couldn't see beyond the long streets of identical houses, the stark high-rise blocks, the lack of bright shops. She didn't know anyone and her neighbours were out all day working, their homes deserted.

Jock fretted about her.

"When you've settled, you could look for a part-time job, too, love."

"Where?" Kirsty snapped back. "Tell me where I could find a job here in this — this brick jungle! For a start I can hardly understand what the folk are saying! A lot of use I'd be in an office!"

True, the local accent was thick and unfamiliar to ears accustomed to the soft, clear speech of Inverness-shire.

Jamie's school looks more like a factory, she wrote to her mother. *All glass and red brick. And it's enormous. Poor wee Jamie must feel really lost, Mum, though he doesn't complain.*

Thank goodness at least he has a nice teacher. Mrs Browning was telling me, when I took Jamie along, that she has cousins in Fort William. So that's always something . . .

Summer and then autumn passed, November arrived along with rain and fog. Every day, Jamie came home for a quick lunch with his mother.

"Nearly everyone stays in school for the lunchbreak," he told her one day. "You get to choose what you like best — baked potatoes and ice cream, Mum."

Kirsty heard the hint of longing in his voice, but would have none of it.

"You'll come home, Jamie. I want to see you in the middle of the day . . . make sure you're OK!"

Jock was working hard and enjoying it, too.

"It's funny being part of such a huge set-up," he told Kirsty. "It's like a world on its own. You should see the big sports complex — squash, swimming, snooker, and a super gym — you name it, they've the lot. It's a real eye-opener after the Kirkmossie place." Jock was smiling and sounded happy.

Kirsty just frowned. First it was Jamie going on about wanting to stay at school for lunch, now it was her husband telling her what a wonderful place this was!

Didn't they realise that every Friday morning her thoughts were back in Kirkmossie, in Rowan Road, having tea and a blether with Mum? Couldn't they see that every Sunday afternoon she just wanted to get ready for high tea with the family?

Now at weekends they just went for walks around the estate.

During one they found an adventure playground for the children . . . swings, roundabouts, rope ladders and a Tarzan treehouse. It was so different to the wee swing-park with its duck pond back home in Kirkmossie. Jamie was so excited he couldn't get into the adventure park fast enough, and they had to drag him away after an hour . . .

EARLY in December, Jock announced there was to be a Christmas Eve party.

"Everyone's invited — Ma, Pa, and the bairns. There's a giant tree and presents for the wee ones. There'll be dancing and a Christmas feast, too. It'll be great."

Kirsty could hardly believe her ears.

"On Christmas Eve we'll be in Kirkmossie. We're not spending Christmas here!"

"Why?" Jock asked with a hint of anger in his voice. "This is our home, isn't it?"

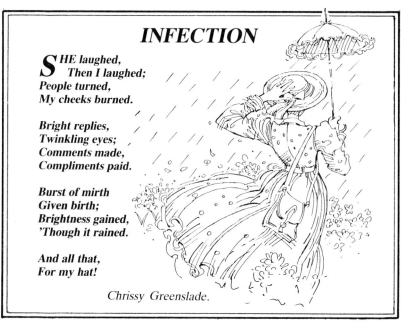

INFECTION

SHE laughed,
*   Then I laughed;*
People turned,
My cheeks burned.

Bright replies,
Twinkling eyes;
Comments made,
Compliments paid.

Burst of mirth
Given birth;
Brightness gained,
'Though it rained.

And all that,
For my hat!

Chrissy Greenslade.

"We always go to my mother's at Christmas. It's a family time. You know that fine."

"Family? Might I remind you that your family's right here at twenty-seven Plumgate Terrace, Birmingham. Me and Jamie!"

"And might I remind you, Jock McLean, that you promised me we'd go back north for all the holidays!"

"Summer holidays, yes. Not Christmas."

"So now you're backing out? Maybe you only made these promises to make sure Jamie and me came away with you."

"That's enough!" Jock exploded. "Hold your tongue.

"I never promised Christmas in Kirkmossie — never! How could I? I'm off on Christmas Day, but that's all. Anyway, even if I could take a week — what about the expense? All the way there in the train and back. We couldn't afford it."

Tears of shock and disappointment filled Kirsty's eyes. Jock had never spoken to her like that before.

But Jock's anger didn't last long. He took out his wallet and handed his wife a bundle of notes.

"Here, Kirsty. Take the bus into Birmingham tomorrow and get yourself something nice to wear to the party."

Kirsty wasn't so ready to forgive and forget. She stuffed the money back into his hands.

"Don't think a new dress is going to make everything all right between us!"

Her husband glared.

"Oh, Kirsty, Kirsty, you're so stubborn, so you are! From the word go, you made up your mind you didn't want to come to Plumgate. You won't even try to like it here. Do what you want!" Jock slammed out of the house.

The very next day a letter arrived from Kirsty's mum.

It's going to be some party with us all together again. I've ordered the turkey and I'm going to make a dumpling this year. The cake was baked last month and Dolly says she'll ice it. And I've made lots of Christmas pies and shortbread, all the tins are full.

Angus says he'll meet you at Inverness, so when will you be arriving?

FOR the first time since they were married, Kirsty and Jock barely spoke to one another. Jock began to work overtime and not come home till late in the evening.

The atmosphere in the house was strained and beginning to tell on wee Jamie. Kirsty found herself snapping at him, or lost in a world of her own, back home in Kirkmossie surrounded by her family.

"Mummy, you're not listening. I'm talking to you! I'm trying to tell you something important," Jamie's voice grew louder as he tried to get his mum's attention.

Kirsty realised Jamie was pulling at her arm. "What was that, Jamie?"

"I was telling you." He was holding out a scrap of paper. "This is

150

for you. Drew gave it to me for you."

"Drew?"

"Drew's my friend at school. He's the same age as me — exactly. We're both six and a half! We even have the same birthdays! Isn't that funny?"

Kirsty was ashamed of herself. Was she so full of self-pity she wasn't listening to her own son?

She gave him a cuddle and read the note.

Will you let Jamie come to tea tomorrow? Drew will bring him here straight from school. You can call around half past eight to take him home.

It was signed Isla Talman, (Drew's mum), 69 Plumgate Boulevard.

The Boulevard? Wasn't that the long street of flatted houses which ran at right-angles to Plumgate Terrace? Kirsty asked Jamie to tell her more.

"I told you and told you, Mummy. Drew's in my class at school, we're best friends.

"Please let me go! Drew has three planes and a helicopter and a real baby in his house. He told me."

Next day after Jamie had left for school, Kirsty looked again at the signature on the note: Isla Talman.

Isla — such a Highland name! Her heart leapt at the possibility that Drew's family had come from Scotland, too.

★　　　★　　　★　　　★

That evening when she left to collect Jamie, Jock hadn't returned from his overtime shift. Kirsty decided there was no need to leave a note; she would be back long before Jock was due home.

As Kirsty rang the bell at the Talmans' house she could hear children's excited voices, shouting and laughter.

A pretty, slim young woman opened the door cràdling a chubby, sleepy infant in her arms.

"Mrs McLean? Oh, hello. Come in, come in. This is Catriona, our baby . . ." Kirsty soon realised that the Talmans certainly weren't Scottish, not with that strange accent!

151

IN THE KITCHEN

With
Anne and John Taylor

QUICK 'N' EASY KEDGEREE

4 oz. (125 g) easy-cook long-grain rice

Salt and pepper, to taste

1 oz. (25 g) butter

1 small onion, chopped

1 teaspoonful curry powder

1 x 200 g can John West Tuna in vegetable oil, drained

2 eggs, hard boiled and chopped

2 tablespoonfuls (30 ml) single cream or plain yoghurt

2 tablespoonfuls fresh parsley, chopped

Cook rice in salted boiling water until tender then drain.

While rice is cooking, melt butter in a large saucepan. Add onion and cook over a medium heat until soft and golden. Stir in curry powder and cook for 30 seconds, remove from heat and stir in rice.

Break up tuna and fold into rice with eggs and cream. Place over a low heat for 2 minutes to heat through then season to taste. Stir in parsley before serving.

BANANA AND COCONUT CAKE

4 oz. (100 g) butter or margarine

4 oz. (100 g) light muscovado sugar

3 eggs, size 3

3 medium bananas, chopped or mashed

6 oz. (175 g) self-raising wholemeal flour

1 oz. (25 g) dessicated coconut

Finely-grated rind of 1 lemon

2 tablespoonfuls (30 ml) milk

Pre-heat oven to 350 deg. F., 180 deg. C., Gas Mark 4. Line a 2-lb. (900-g) loaf tin with non-stick paper.

Cream together the butter and sugar until light, then beat in the eggs. Beat in the bananas, then fold in the flour, coconut and lemon rind. Mix in the milk to a soft dropping consistency, then turn into the tin and level the surface. Bake for about 1 hour, until firm and golden. Turn out and cool on a wire rack.

Serves 4.

POACHERS ROLL

1 lb. (450 g) pork sausagemeat

1 cooking apple, peeled, cored and grated

4 oz. (100 g) sweetcorn

1 teaspoonful chopped, fresh or dried tarragon

Salt and pepper, to taste

12 oz. (300 g) shortcrust pastry

1 egg, beaten

To Serve. —
Crisp salad

Pre-heat oven to 375 deg. F., 190 deg. C., Gas Mark 5.

Mix together the sausagemeat, apple, sweetcorn, herbs and seasoning.

Roll out the pastry to an oblong approx. 10 inches x 11 inches (25 cm x 27 cm). Spread the filling ingredients over the pastry to within an inch of the edge. Brush around the edge with beaten egg and roll up the pastry as for a sausage roll. Place on a baking sheet, brush with beaten egg, use any trimmings for decoration on top of the roll and in turn brush with the egg.

Bake in the centre of oven for 45 minutes or until golden and cooked. Serve cold, cut into slices with a crisp salad.
Serves 4.

RASPBERRY PANCAKE LAYER

12 oz. (350 g) raspberries

½ pint (300 ml) double cream, whipped

1 dessertspoonful caster sugar

6 wholemeal pancakes

To Decorate. —
A few raspberries, optional

A little whipped cream, optional

Fold raspberries, cream and sugar together. Layer pancakes with raspberry cream. Decorate with raspberries and piped cream, if liked.

Anne's Tip:—
This can be made with ordinary pancakes — home-made are best!

153

The living-room was in a mess. Toys, cushions and books were scattered around and there was a tent made out of an old bedcover draped across two chairs.

Jamie and his friend, Drew, crouched at the entrance of it with feathers stuck in their hair and sticks in their hands. A little boy who Kirsty thought was about three years old, was ready to dive from the back of the couch . . .

"Sit down if you can find space." Drew's mother had to shout to be heard above the general din.

"Wait till I put Catriona to bed — her eyes are just about closed, then I'll make us a cup of tea and we can have a chat. OK?"

Kirsty was intrigued. Isla — Catriona — Drew, short for Andrew of course, and the wee boy . . . Hadn't someone called him Colin? Such Scottish names. And living here in Plumgate!

Isla Talman was back in a minute.

"It's great when Catriona settles so quickly. With any luck she'll sleep now till six tomorrow.

"Come into the kitchen. We'll have a bit of peace there. Right, boys, time to clear up. All toys back in their boxes — now!"

She shut the kitchen door and switched on the kettle. Taking out two mugs and a plate of biscuits, then she turned to Kirsty.

"Well, how are you settling in, Mrs McLean? Jamie tells us you've not been here long."

"Kirsty — please call me Kirsty." She avoided the young woman's straight blue gaze.

"Settling? I'm not. I don't like Plumgate. I — I really hate the place. We, that is Jock and me, come from the north, beyond Inverness."

"Inverness? Well, what do you know! That's where my great-grandparents were born! They emigrated way back in — oh, just after World War One, I think. We're proud of our Scottish roots — that's why we decided to give our children Scottish names."

"I noticed. I wondered about that."

"You'll have guessed we're from New Zealand. From Warra Springs — you'll never have heard of that place, I bet? Take a mug and help yourself to biscuits.

"We had warm springs shooting up close to our garden . . . just the thing for lazing in or swimming. The climate was perfect — there were palm trees and big tropical flowers growing beside our home.

"When I was young my folk had a sheep station and I rode to school on horseback. It was a good life all right. I've some pictures of Warra Springs. Would you like to see them, Kirsty?" Without waiting for an answer, Isla Talman hurried away to fetch them.

Kirsty had listened in growing wonderment. How could Isla Talman speak so casually, so lightheartedly, about what she'd left behind? How could she accept Plumgate with its flatness, the miles of streets and stale city air?

"But tell me," she asked as soon as her new friend appeared. "Why on earth did you come here?"

"Allan's work. He's a jeweller, trained to make rings and bracelets and all sorts. Not the real thing but for the costume jewellery market.

"He had his own business in Warra but it failed and we were left without anything. Then he found out there were plenty of openings for his kind of work in England, here in Birmingham. So — here we are! Look, I'll show you these photographs . . ."

An hour and a half later it was little Colin who brought the two young mums back to earth. The wee lad came roaring into the kitchen complaining the big boys wouldn't let him play any more!

Kirsty looked in dismay at her wristwatch. It was nearly ten o'clock. She rushed to get Jamie's coat. But Isla still carried on chatting.

"I'm on my own with the children all this week because Allan had to go to London. There are times I get fed up being on my own. I'd love to get into the city to do some Christmas shopping, but it's not so easy when I've got to take three youngsters along with me."

"I'll take the bairns off your hands for a day, Isla," Kirsty found herself offering. "I'd like to have them — I really would."

"That would be super. You don't know what you're letting yourself in for, but thank you just the same!" And they both laughed.

Kirsty and Jamie quickly said their goodbyes to their friends and left to hurry home. Outside in the street it was very dark and quiet.

WHEN Kirsty and Jamie reached their own gate they ran full tilt into a figure looming out of the darkness.

"Oh, Jock! It's you! You gave us a fright!"

"I gave you a fright! What sort of a fright do you think you've given me? Coming home to a dark empty house and no message to say where you were. Where have you been, the pair of you?"

Jock McLean had been so badly worried. Well, with him and Kirsty barely speaking to one another recently . . . he'd actually believed they must have left him and run off back to Kirkmossie for Christmas!

Over supper, Kirsty told Jock about the Talman family, how friendly Isla had been and where they'd lived before coming to Plumgate.

"New Zealand! And they're so happy here. It's amazing when you think where they used to live . . ."

He came round the table to take her in his strong arms.

"Listen to me! Happiness isn't about streets and houses and places. It's about people. It's about being close to the ones you love and care most about, no matter where.

"Your new friend knows that. Plumgate — New Zealand — Kirkmossie — they don't matter if the one you love and the children you love are with you."

Kirsty reached on tip-toe to cling to him. Now she felt safe, secure, and able, at long last, to put Kirkmossie behind her and look forward to a new future with her family and new friends. □

SISTERS UNDER

IT was lunchtime before I began sorting out the mail I'd grabbed as I'd left the flat that morning. I'd been too tired even to look at the heap on the mat the previous evening. My flight had been delayed and my only thought had been to get to bed.

I knew I ought to call Poppy to thank her for the airmail letters she'd sent me while I was abroad. I felt a stab of guilt, thinking of the short, apologetic postcards I'd sent in return, pleading the pressure of work to make up for the economy of words.

How had Poppy coped alone these last three months since our mother's death? Her letters were cheerful open and friendly — so like Poppy — yet betrayed a little loneliness. What an elder sister I'd turned out to be. I sighed. I should have been able to give her comfort, yet I'd always been afraid to express my feelings.

"How would you like a sister, Claire?" Mum asked, when I was ten.

I was overjoyed, thinking she meant a baby. She looked relieved. Then she told me they were hoping to adopt someone called Poppy who was four years old.

THE SKIN

by
**ALISON
WHITE**

It was a total shock. I'd thought we were a happy family, so why did they want this Poppy?

"Poppy has had a bad time," Mum explained. "She's lost both her parents. We'd like to love her and make her happy again. You'd like someone to play with wouldn't you, Claire?"

The day Poppy came, Mum and Dad fussed over me, saying how much they loved me. It was reassuring yet unsettling, too.

I was fascinated by Poppy. Her hair was blonde and in long curls that sprang around her head and bounced on her shoulders. She wore a white dress with red cats on and red tights. I'll never forget that first impression of her. Everything about her was bright and fizzy.

157

The phone on my desk rang, bringing me back to the present.

"Hi, Claire, it's Poppy. How does it feel to be back?"

"Great! I was just thinking about you."

"Oh dear!" She paused. "I suppose you've got the letter from Mum's solicitor?"

"I haven't opened everything yet," I admitted.

"It's just to say her estate is settled and asking when we can sign the paperwork."

"Well, I was planning to see you anyway. How about next Friday?" I suggested.

"Fine. You'll stay for the weekend?"

"Possibly." I was reluctant to commit myself. "I'll come down Thursday evening."

POPPY and I had never been close. I suppose deep down I'd been jealous. She was the one who had been *chosen.*

The age difference didn't help. At four, Poppy was almost a toddler, whilst I at ten, considered myself worldly wise.

We were such different characters, too. I was quiet and reserved, whereas Poppy was lively and full of fun.

"I'm so lucky to be here," she'd said once, referring to her adoption.

I'd lost my temper and she'd never mentioned it again. But I knew she lived by an unwritten rule, that I, the natural daughter, should always come first.

Mum never pushed us together but taught us to respect one another, accepting our differences. She loved us equally but I couldn't help feeling that she laughed more with Poppy. Looking back, it was surprising Mum coped at all — especially as we lost Dad when I was sixteen. Maybe the two of us kept her going.

At eighteen, I'd left for university and, with my sights set on a career, visited home only occasionally. Poppy was always pleased to see me and so full of questions that I found it overwhelming and ended up being less friendly than I'd intended.

After Poppy finished school she studied Art and Textiles at a college nearby, so stayed home even then.

"Claire . . . something awful has happened."

Those words were etched on my mind, since Poppy had spoken them three months ago.

Mum had died suddenly. I was working abroad and got a flight home as soon as I could. Poppy had coped marvellously for someone so young. She was only twenty-two.

Together we made the necessary arrangements. I felt guilty and sad that I hadn't spent more time with Mum.

"None of us could have known, Claire," Poppy said tentatively, the night after the funeral. "So don't feel bad."

"I'm sad," I snapped. "That's natural."

It was guilt talking, but Poppy blushed and drew back as though I'd slapped her.

I'd been restless, unable to grieve, and was almost grateful when the bank called with a problem.

"You must go," Poppy insisted.

"But it's the project I set up overseas. If I go back, it'll be three months till I can come home."

"Oh! Well, you must still go, Claire. It's your job. Nothing's happening here — the solicitor says things will take time."

"Will you be OK?" I asked. "I feel as though I'm abandoning you."

"Rubbish," she said briskly. "I'm fine." She hesitated. "You'll keep in touch though, won't you?"

I'd left the next day. And Poppy was a lot better than me at keeping in touch. I'd kept her letters, they'd been fun to read, and somehow made me feel closer to her — and even to Mum.

A ND now I was going home again. At least for a day or so. I took the train, rather than drive, and I was glad to escape the noise and heat of the city.

I remembered train journeys with Mum and Poppy . . . me buried in a book, Poppy chattering all the way, Mum's voice a gentle murmur in the background.

Home was only five minutes' walk from the station. Memories washed over me as I made my way down the lane, listening to the shouts of the boys playing in the field.

I turned the corner and saw the house of my childhood. The sandstone looked mellow in the fading light.

Poppy must have been looking out for me, for the front door opened and she came running down the path.

"Claire!" She wore a casual shirt and skirt and no make-up, yet had a vibrant natural beauty.

She flung the gate open and threw her arms around me.

"You look great!"

"Thanks."

I touched my hair self-consciously. Rigid with hairspray, it seemed ridiculously confined compared with her blonde tangle of coppery curls. My dress, too, so smart in the city, seemed out of place here.

"Coffee's ready."

Poppy led me through the house.

"I've vamped the kitchen up a bit — only a tin of varnish though, hope you don't mind."

The kitchen units had been stained antique pine, giving the room a honeyed glow. Pots, pans and dried flowers hung from a rack on the ceiling, and Poppy's sewing was scattered everywhere.

"It's great. So, what's new? Busy?"

"Mmm. I've got a deal with a couple of stores in town now, doing curtains and stuff."

"You'll have to take on outworkers," I suggested, "and get orders from the London stores."

"That's the high-flying banker in you talking, Claire. Look at you — you just scream organisation, where I spell chaos."

I laughed.

"I think it's decreed early on in life. I mean I could never be called Poppy, could I? Plain old Claire, that's me."

"Poppy the hippy, that's me." She grinned. "You're right, it's probably decided at birth." She looked serious then and I was afraid she'd think I meant to draw attention to the fact that we weren't natural sisters.

She smiled again.

"Perhaps I'll think about expanding, though."

"You must."

I SUPPOSE while you're here, Claire, you'll be sorting out Mum's clothes and things?"

I frowned.

"What do you mean?"

"Well . . ." she faltered. "If you remember, we didn't want to face it after the funeral."

"You mean you haven't done anything with them yourself?"

Poppy shook her head.

"Why, for heaven's sake?"

"Well — I just didn't think it was my place," she said at last.

"Oh, Poppy!" I cried. "She was your mother, too."

"Yes . . . but, Claire, it's only right that *you* make any decisions."

"Rubbish!" I snorted. "You have every right, just as much as I. This house is yours, for goodness' sake."

"Well, I know that's what Mum suggested, but this has been your home too, and I'm worried —"

"Well, don't be. It's what Mum wanted. She loved us both and treated us fairly in her will. Fifty-fifty. You love this house — have it. I don't want it, OK?"

"OK," she said quietly. "I'm sorry."

"Stop saying that," I snapped. "Oh . . . I'm sorry, Poppy. It's just — well, being in the house again. And it's been a long week. Maybe I need to wind down a bit. I'll start looking through her things and later we'll bag them up together. All right?"

"Fine." She smiled and took the empty cups over to the sink.

Feeling lousy, I went upstairs.

I picked up the photo by Mum's bed.

Mum, Dad, me and Poppy, all laughing. Now it was only Poppy and me, and Poppy obviously didn't feel like part of the family any more. Had I really made her feel that unwelcome? That lonely? I'd never wanted that, but somehow had never been able to tell her how I'd really felt.

I'd apologise later for snapping. She was only doing what she thought was right, still grieving for Mum.

I'd tried to organise my life so I wouldn't have time to think too much, and I hadn't given myself a chance to grieve . . .

Mum's clothes were neatly hung and folded, but there was the usual disarray of junk at the bottom of the wardrobe. I pulled out an oddly-shaped bag.

INSIDE, were two hats and I recognised them instantly. Poppy and I had worn them to my cousin's wedding five years ago. Mine, a pillbox to match my suit. Poppy, seventeen and just started at art college, had worn a multi-layered dress in green with a ludicrous hat of green crushed velvet, its wide floppy brim rolled up in front and secured with a cluster of lush, red fabric poppies. It was quite ridiculous, yet she had looked beautiful.

As I looked at the hats, I realised why Mum had kept them. They seemed to sum up the very essence of our personalities. Mine, simple and safe, Poppy's outrageous and brave.

Slowly turning Poppy's hat in my hands, I moved to the mirror and put it on. It was then that I started to cry — all the pain I'd been bottling up inside me at last being released with my tears. I hadn't faced my loss properly yet. And now, through my inability to communicate, it looked as though I might lose Poppy, too.

I heard a noise and turned. Poppy stood in the doorway, holding two mugs of coffee. She put them down on the bedside cabinet.

"I'm sorry, Claire. You're right. I should have made a start on the sorting out."

"No —" I began, but my voice broke.

"It's funny," Poppy said softly, "but when I found the hats, I put yours on. Daft, isn't it?"

"Yours is nicer."

"Yours is sophisticated. I wish — I've always wished — I could be more like you, Claire."

"But I've always wanted to be more like you."

We stared at each other for a moment.

"Mum had it right," Poppy said. "She loved us both for what we are."

I nodded.

"I've not been much of a sister to you, Poppy. I didn't seem able to get to know you. You were right about grieving, though, I don't think I've finished yet. I can't seem to handle it."

"I know," she murmured. "I know."

She picked up my hat, and studied it.

"Funny it should be these that got us talking honestly, isn't it? Maybe Mum wanted us to find them."

Absently, she put my hat on and looked in the mirror, then at the photo on the bedside table. Her eyes filled with tears.

"I'm sorry, Claire." She sniffed.

"Oh, Poppy!" I held out my arms and the next moment I was hugging her close.

"We still have each other," Poppy whispered. And she was right. Maybe we were sisters where it really mattered most. *Underneath* the skin. ☐

L

NELL McRAY brushed the flour off her hands with a sigh of relief. She was glad to have the shortbread safely in the oven. Her hands were really getting a bit too stiff to do it now. This really would have to be the last time she made it. But Claire, her daughter-in-law, always seemed so pleased to get it, all the same . . .

She thought of the preparations that would be going on at her son's house. It would be decorated from top to bottom. The Christmas tree would soar up to the ceiling in the hall, presents would be piled everywhere, and Claire would be calmly and efficiently presiding over it all.

An Old-

I don't know how she does it, thought Nell. Especially with the baby due in a few days.

She was glad to remember that Claire's mother would be up from England to help, nearer the time.

Nell made herself a cup of tea and sat down in the old rocking chair to enjoy it.

Tomorrow would be Christmas Day.

She'd have to get dressed up for the party. It seemed rather ingrateful to think that she'd rather spend the day quietly here.

She'd never been used to hustle and bustle. The little two-room flat where she lived now was similar to the one she'd grown up in. Somehow, she had never aspired to anything more when she and Dave were married. "Our little but an' ben," she'd called it, and they couldn't have been happier in a palace.

When Scott was born, they'd talked about a house and garden, but the years passed and they were still there when Dave had that fatal heart attack.

After that, it had been a struggle, with ten-year-old Scott to bring up on her own, but Nell had made it.

Now Scott had a good job. He and Claire could afford the big house, and with five-year old Susie and three-year-old Heather it was a perfect home.

Nell had just started to tidy away her baking things when the doorbell rang. She was astonished to find Scott standing there — with Heather in his arms and Susie beside him!

"What on earth's wrong?" she asked anxiously, knowing that he

Fashioned
Christmas

by MARION STEWART

163

was usually at the office at this time of the morning.

"It's Claire," he said quickly. "She's had a dizzy spell and I've had to take her to the hospital."

"Is she hurt? Is it the baby?" asked Nell, absolutely shocked.

"No, no — nobody's hurt," said Scott, "but Claire began to feel there was something wrong and that she'd better get to the hospital. Can you keep the girls, Mother? I have to go to the hospital. I'll call in later and let you know how she is."

"Of course, of course! Come on in, girls. Off you go, Scott. Well, hurry!"

Scott stammered his goodbyes. The little girls took off their coats, chattering excitedly after their father had gone.

"She was in the front room," Susie explained. "There was a bit of holly she said was squint so she stretched up to straighten it out and she nearly fell."

The girls fell silent. Of course, they were worried. Especially Susie, who felt quite protective towards Heather as the wee one ran her fingers over the floury board.

"Can I bake something?" Susie asked, eager to see her sister doing something, even if it was only helping to cook.

"Me, too," said Heather, dragging up a stool to stand on. "I can bake!"

Nell thought for a minute. It suddenly occurred to her that she had nothing to keep the girls entertained all day! Perhaps baking a few biscuits would be as good a way as any to keep the children occupied! Yes! She got the ingredients out, and an hour flew by as the threesome patted dough into weird shapes, and made eyes of currants and mouths of orange peel, chattering all the time. Everything that might turn out edible was put in the oven — the shortbread having been removed — and the kitchen was tidied before a start was made on lunch.

THEY had just finished their sandwiches when Scott arrived, and such news! Claire was all right — but the baby was liable to be born at any minute!

"I must get back to the hospital," he said, all of a dither. "Could you keep the children here, Mother, or would you like me to take you all to the house?"

The girls clamoured to stay.

"Of course, we're getting on fine here!" And Nell meant it.

A few very peculiar biscuits later, Heather eagerly asked, "Can we sleep in Daddy's bed?"

It always seemed to amuse them that Daddy had slept in the "wall-bed" in the parlour when he was a boy. She agreed, so when Scott had gone they helped Nell to make it up.

"I'll need to look out nightdresses for you," she said, and they helped her pull out the heavy drawers in the big chest, giggling as Nell tried on various bed-jackets to find something to fit the little bodies.

"Will Santa know we're here?" asked Heather. Suddenly Nell remembered that it was Christmas Eve. She'd forgotten in all the hustle and bustle of the day.

"Yes, dearie," she said. "But we'll have to hang up our stockings so he can be quite sure!"

She hunted out some heavy stockings, and they were duly hung up at the fireplace. Then they spent the afternoon quietly, playing with boxes of old postcards, tiddlywinks and snakes and ladders. After all, Nell didn't have any modern, plastic toys. The girls really enjoyed themselves, all the same.

Nell, thinking of Scott's large, spacious home, with all the children's presents waiting to be opened, was worried that the girls would be bored and unhappy. But even the scene from her big front window, looking on to the street, with the snow falling and the lights in the shops shining on the crowds of last-minute shoppers seemed to fascinate them.

"Can we get in the big bath?" asked Susie as Nell started setting the table for tea.

In no time, they were having a hilarious time in Nell's big, old-fashioned tub.

Then it was tea and boiled eggs.

With the fire flickering warmly behind the fire-screen, the girls were tucked up in the wall-bed under the old patchwork quilt. Nell read them Christmas stories till they fell asleep.

Several times during the night, she crept in to see that they were all right and early in the morning she laid the stockings at the front of the bed, plump and heavy now with the little gifts she had found to fill them.

When it was time to get up, Nell heard squeals of delight coming from the room. She went to join in the fun of emptying the stockings. There were lace-edged handkerchiefs, little cakes of soap, a pencil each, a coin and some sweets and, of course, an apple and an orange — and a piece of shortbread!

Susie and Heather still hadn't dressed by the time Scott arrived.

There was no need to ask if all was well. His face shone with relief — and happiness.

"You have a little brother," he said as he kissed the girls. "A grandson, Mother."

"And Claire?" asked Nell.

"Good," he said. "Just a bit tired, now."

He lifted the girls into his arms.

"Have you been good girls?" he asked.

"Oh, yes, Daddy," they cried, their voices tumbling over each other as they told him about their stay and asked about the new arrival.

"Oh, Daddy, this has been the best Christmas we've ever had in our lives," said Susie, pure contentment radiating from her eyes.

Nell gave a sigh of relief.

The simple life had its good points still, she thought happily. □

WHEN THE FUTURE BECKONS

W HEN Em learned that Rod was back, it conjured up a lot of warming images for her, of the years when their families lived in adjoining cottages by the river.

Rod Drewe had been fun. Some ten years older than her, he had already been working as a trainee surveyor when she was at the junior school, yet they struck up a friendship which spanned childhood to manhood.

Rod nicknamed her "Whippersnapper" because she was smaller, and she nicknamed him "Grizzly", from those few rare occasions he hadn't warmed to her childhood pranks.

Yet usually he joined in — tweaking her bunches or stealing her comics, and sharing confidences in their "den," which was really a pine bench under the curtain of weeping willow by the river-bank.

Here they would have serious discussions about wide-ranging issues, from whether people should be made to eat brussels sprouts, to whether eleven-year-olds really *should* be made to go to bed by 9.30 p.m.

Rod shared laughter at her birthday candles, and comforted her over the loss of Oscar, her pet rabbit.

His favourite trick had been to hoist her on to his shoulders.

"So you can see farther than I can, Em!" he would tease.

Of course, she couldn't see more, for she had been only a child.

It came as quite a shock to her to hear her mother's news.

"Getting married? Rod?" she had echoed, thinking Rod had always treated her as his best friend.

She had felt hurt and let-down, but of course she *had* been only a child and Rod had then been twenty-one and madly in love with a girl called Karen.

Rod married his Karen and moved away, while Em — simply grew up . . .

S O Rod was back, yet Em gave it only a passing thought that morning. Well, she did have a backlog of typing for the office manager, and Rod was a cosy memory from her childhood, nothing more.

"Rod's back," her mother told her over their evening meal, it seemed for the umpteenth time that day.

They still lived in the cottages by the river, Em with her parents,

166

by SUZANNA NIX

although Rod's mum was now widowed.

"It seems he's got a new job here — and a divorce, too," her mother went on, as if the two went together.

That got Em's attention. Poor Rod! How could someone so warm and caring end up divorced? Well, whatever the reason, she was sure Rod was just the person to cope.

After all, Rod had always had the answers for everything and a smile even in the greatest adversity. Yet when Em stepped out into the garden for a breath of the June evening, it was quite a different Rod Drewe she found brooding by the river-bank. But then, she had forgotten that time hadn't stood still for either of them . . .

Of course he looked just the same, physically. That wavy brown hair, just ever so slightly tousled, those broad shoulders and the casual shirt and jeans were all the Rod Em knew and remembered.

Yet when he turned from his sombre thoughts, his drawn expression wasn't the Rod she had known and certainly not the one she remembered.

His face first registered surprise, then disbelief.

"Em? It isn't Emma, is it?"

She laughed softly. "Yes, Rod, it is!"

His initial surprise passed, and he gave her a stiff smile and paid her an equally stiff compliment.

"You've — er — changed. You look great."

Em nodded dully, for this wasn't the Rod she remembered. It took a moment to pin-point the difference. Then it was clear — this man was angry.

"Will you be living here, with your mother?" she asked, more to fill the awkward silence than out of a genuine curiosity.

"Yes, at least until I find a place of my own," Rod answered, rather disinterestedly.

"I was sorry to hear about your divorce," Em said, to fill that awkward silence again.

For a moment he looked cautious, as if he hadn't realised she knew, then forced a tight smile.

"So how are things with you, Whippersnapper?"

Rod pronounced the old nickname with relish, as if it were a magic word and by saying it he could lighten the mood and evade her efforts at real communication, Em thought in exasperation —

What did he expect — that at the mention of it she would tie her hair into bunches and cartwheel around the lawn?

I'VE grown a little, I think, since those days," she replied coolly. He looked away to the river uncomfortably.

"I'm sorry if you thought I was probing, Rod," she went on. "I thought it might help to talk, that was all."

He looked back at her, narrowing his eyes as if unable to see for the glint of the sun reflecting off the water.

"We grew apart — or so my wife said. We ended up like strangers — and she found someone else." P 170 ▶

Historic Scotland

BANNOCKBURN

A S every scholar knows, or ought to know, the Battle of Bannockburn was fought in the year 1314, and in it King Robert the Bruce, with his army of 5,500, triumphed over Edward II of England's army of 20,000 men.

By careful planning, good leadership and great courage, the Scots won a classic victory, and Bannockburn is rightly included among the decisive battles of history.

A pre-battle incident will always be remembered. Bruce was riding on a pony in front of his army, when an English knight, Sir Henry de Bohun, recognising him by his gold coronet, thought he could bring an end to the battle before it had begun. So, on his great war-horse and with lance couched, he rode upon Bruce at full speed.

The King turned his pony, avoiding the thrust of the lance, and, rising in his stirrups, he felled de Bohun with a mighty blow of his battle-axe.

The Scottish leaders chided Bruce for thus exposing himself to danger, but all he said was, "I have broken my good battle-axe."

The battlefield, now in the care of the National Trust for Scotland, lies in a triangular level near Stirling Castle, and between the River Forth and the Bannock Burn.

In 1964 (the 650th anniversary of the battle), a 20 foot high mounted statue of Bruce, sculped by Pilkington Jackson, was set up at the Borestane. This, by tradition, is where Bruce made his headquarters and flew the Scottish Royal Standard.

As an immediate result of the battle, the garrison in Stirling Castle (the last Scottish castle in the hands of the English) surrendered, and Scotland achieved her freedom and independence.

Rod spoke sharply, almost condescendingly, as if to imply Em couldn't hope to understand.

"Well, I can see I'm wasting my time — I mean, I can't hope to understand these grown-up things!" she retorted. "If you'll excuse me, I have to go and put my dolls to bed!"

She caught the glint of a surprised look in his face as she turned and left, and felt, too, an equally acute pang of regret. Rod Drewe, the person she had known and loved, no longer really existed.

That night in her room, though, she couldn't help but think of Rod, next door and no doubt like her trying to find sleep. How sad that life could do that to him and to his memory, blended into her mind like a ray of unforgotten sunshine.

"So you can see more than I can, Em!" She remembered his words, when he had hoisted her on to his shoulders. Well, maybe she couldn't see farther than he had then, but what about now?

Em felt as if Rod were wearing blinkers while she could see clearly. Rod was lost in self-pity and unless someone told him that, he might never find happiness again.

Yet how could she ever hope to help him? It was clear from their little chat — or attempted chat — in the garden that evening, that Rod still thought of her as a child. Until he saw her as the young woman she was, it was unlikely he would take her seriously over anything.

EM found a way to help Rod, though, the very next day, even if it was only to pick him up at the bus-stop by the village green.

"Want a lift?" she offered from her car window.

For a moment he looked uncomfortable.

"I sold my car," he explained, "because my new job gives me a company one — only I don't get it until I start next week."

Em, in turn, shrugged and gave him a sweet smile, opening the passenger door for him. She supposed it was slightly difficult for him to accept — the little girl from next door offering him a lift in her car . . .

As she headed for the main road and the route to town, she noticed Rod was glancing at her. She realised what that uncomfortable little feeling was that had spread between them like glue the previous

P 172 ▶

KELSO

*T*HE *town's spectacular ruined abbey was built early in the 12th century for monks from Chartres, but was largely destroyed four hundred years later. Kelso is busy with visitors, attracting many fishermen to the famous rivers of the Teviot and Tweed. That well-loved Borders figure, Sir Walter Scott, attended the old grammar school, now no more, in 1738.*

KELSO : J CAMPBELL KERR

evening — Rod was attracted to her.

So he *had* seen her as a woman after all, and more unnerving still was the realisation she was attracted to him. She no longer saw him as the older boy from next door who made her laugh, but as quite an eligible proposition — if it hadn't been for his frown and grouchiness.

"Rod, I hope you won't think I'm prying. I really *was* sorry to hear about your divorce," Em tried again.

"Well, it's something you have to experience really, to know what it's like," Rod said.

There it was again, Em thought, the bitterness, the condescending tone. She stifled a sigh and changed into a higher gear.

"I don't think you always have to experience something to share someone's loss," she reminded him, trying to keep her voice and her irritation under control.

"I remember when my rabbit, Oscar, died. I remember you sat in the den with me and cried, too — if only inwardly. I could tell."

She glanced over at him and saw that memory chase over his face, too. For a moment it dissolved in tenderness before he replied, rather curtly, "Divorce is more than a lost rabbit."

Em fought back a wave of anger. She just wished she hadn't reminded him of the child he obviously still thought she was.

"Drop me off here, would you?" Rod asked.

"Here?" Em echoed, surprised.

"This is the company I'll be working for."

Em looked up at the tall office-block ahead of them.

"Thanks for the lift," Rod said as he reached for the door.

"Rod?"

He turned back to her and Em knew it was too late — she wasn't going to be able to keep her angry feelings to herself.

"It probably *isn't* any of my business and you probably *don't* think I know what I'm talking about, but I think you're wallowing in self-pity — in 'what-might-have-beens'.

"If you don't pull yourself together," she went on in a rush, "you're going to smother your real self and some really good prospects. And if you're wondering what all that has to do with me — Rod Drewe happened to be a man I knew once and liked!"

There, she thought, she had raised her voice and embarrassing tears weren't far behind.

Rod was looking at her quite blankly.

"Have you finished?" he asked, shaken.

Em took a deep breath and steadied herself.

"No, no I haven't! I'm *not* a kid any more, Rod, and you can't just hoist me on your shoulders out of the way! Funny, though, I can still see more than you . . ."

Rod's face softened, breaking into a helpless sort of boyish grin. Then he shook his head.

"I don't think you're a kid, Emma, but it wouldn't be a bad thing if you were — you were really sweet then! Goodbye!"

With that he got out, shut the door, and marched off.

Em took a moment to calm herself, then drove off. That was the last time she would ever offer Rod Drewe either a lift or some advice!

ALL through her day at the office, memories came tumbling back of Whippersnapper and Grizzly. It seemed wrong — a waste — a shame, that two people who had at least been good friends couldn't get on together.

Em felt that the eleven-year-old with the bunches was still very much there inside her, even though her smiling Rod had gone, it seemed, for ever.

Rod hadn't gone for ever, though, as she was to find when she arrived home that evening.

"These came for you — delivered this afternoon!" her mother told her excitedly as she handed over a bouquet.

For a moment, Em was puzzled until she read the card: "To Whippersnapper from Grizzly — see you in the den?"

Her mother looked quite surprised when Em flung down her bag and ran out to the garden, or, more precisely, to Whippersnapper and Grizzly's den.

Rod was there. Maybe it was the sunlight, but he looked lighter — happier.

"Em!" he greeted her. "I want to apologise. I was pretty rotten to you today. I'm sorry and you were right — I've been wallowing in self-pity and it's time I got my act together."

Em's heart and memory flipped, for it was almost as if Rod was back, exactly the same as before.

Yet she knew, neither of them could ever be the same again.

"I — er — I also wanted to ask you out to dinner," Rod went on, biting his lip as if he were nervous — nervous of her, of little Whippersnapper!

"I'd like that, Rod."

"Good!" He grinned. "And I'll even let you drink wine — if you're good, of course!"

Em was about to protest that she *wasn't* a child any more when she realised Rod was teasing, but he was really making fun of himself, of his inability to accept her growing up.

"Well, OK, but only if we can toast to the future," Em cautioned, a mischievous smile on her lips.

Rod smiled, too.

"It's a deal!" He offered her his hand to join him, and as they sat by the river reminiscing, Em knew that Whippersnapper and Grizzly would always be there, in their hearts and memories, even when she and Rod ventured into the future together . . . □

Printed and published in Great Britain by D. C. Thomson & Co., Ltd., Dundee, Glasgow and London. © D. C. Thomson & Co., Ltd., 1995. While every reasonable care will be taken, neither D. C. Thomson & Co., Ltd., nor its agents will accept liability for loss or damage to colour transparencies or any other material submitted to this publication.

ISBN 0-85116-586-9
European Article Number 9-780851 165868

IVELET BRIDGE, SWALEDALE : J CAMPBELL KERR